the
VALEDICTORIANS

To Ryan

As someone roughly the same
age as these characters, I'd like to
imagine you can comprehend their motivations
better than myself. But, whether or not that
is the case, I think you'll find this an
entertaining tale of loss and disillusionment.
As I said, writing this helped me a great
deal in my own life, and I hope
you'll find it relevant to your own
post-collegiate existence.

Much Love - Brook

the
VALEDICTORIANS

MITCH COTE-CROSSKILL

MILL CITY PRESS

MINNEAPOLIS, MN

Mill City Press, Inc.
212 3rd Avenue North, Suite 290
Minneapolis, MN 55401
612.455.2294
www.millcitypublishing.com

ISBN - 978-1-936107-36-0
ISBN - 1-936107-36-8
LCCN - 2009941713

Cover Design and Typeset by Melanie Shellito

Printed in the United States of America

For my fellow Valedictorians and for Sandie.

Man, that dog knew how to have a good time.

1

RISE TO A NEW DAY

I KNEW WHEN I woke up that doing so was a mistake. It always was.

Lightning shot up my side, involuntarily flipping my eyelids open against the pre-dawn light sifting through my window's blinds. The brightness entered through my eyes and ricocheted off the walls of my skull. I flinched and desperately wished I was still unconscious. Realizing that was not an option, I slowly allowed my brain to grasp the facts. I was lying on the hardwood floor of my bedroom, my face pressed into a sticky puddle of my drool. Squeezed between my torso and the floor was a half-finished handle of vodka. I fought to raise my head and, exhausted, let it drop again. I was freezing, and it quickly became clear why. I was naked from the waist down. Still had my socks on though, which was key. I hated having cold feet. Cold feet are the kind of thing that can ruin a good night's sleep.

I glanced down and realized something else. I was wearing a condom, its unfamiliar latex length crumpled up on the tip of my now shrunken phallus. I stared at my penis with a sort of detached amusement, realizing now more than ever it was self-delusion when man imagined himself ruler of his own sexuality. It, unlike us, never rested, and now because of it my morning was complicated. A muffled snore echoed from my bed, confirming the trouble on my horizon.

I propped myself up on my elbow and reached over to grab a pair of boxers lying near me. After I had slid them on I blinked a couple of times and smacked my lips softly, steeling myself for the inevitable. The pounding in my head threatened to chase out any potential thoughts, but I focused and tried to formulate one. I needed to see who was sleeping in my bed. Then I should get a glass of water. I crawled over to the corner of my mattress and for the first time I noticed how absurd my sheets were. Pink and white flowers on a baby blue backdrop. My parents' sheets for my parents' bed. I'd had them for a couple of years now and had never given them a real look. Funny how you missed the obvious like that. Another thought hit me. I had, in all likelihood, been conceived in the same twenty-five-year-old mattress I myself was now having sex in. A mildly disturbing observation. Maybe I could buy some new sheets today.

A soft snort snapped me out of my reverie. Body tensed, I slowly let my head rise up over the side of my bed. My wide eyes quickly discovered a female form. Phew. You never knew. If I had as much to drink as I suspected I'd had, it was entirely possible I had found myself a young man with a delicate bone structure and convinced myself I had hit jackpot. Thankfully, it appeared otherwise. She faced away, hiding her face while exposing the majority of her body. Looking across that field of flowers, I soaked it in. She looked to be rather tall, with a mildly voluptuous frame. Clad in only underwear, I saw nicely toned legs melding seamlessly into a pleasantly rounded butt. I couldn't help feel a little voyeuristic ogling her while she slept, but I had to assume we had done much worse last night. Above her posterior I found the smooth ivory skin of her back, which disappeared under a mane of ebony hair. Her sides rhythmically rose and fell as she inhaled and exhaled the cool morning air, and I saw her unconsciously pull the thin sheet she was holding a little closer to her body.

For a brief instant I forgot my hangover and allowed myself to be fascinated by the situation. I didn't often have ladies sleeping over in my bed, mostly because I, especially of late, was getting too sloppy to be able to talk to girls when I went out. I'd heard from my buddies I was a riot between eight and ten, but by the time we hit the bars I usually ended up somewhere between blackout and comatose. This is how I preferred myself.

But somehow, some way, I had managed to keep it together long enough to woo a member of the opposite sex. Or maybe she had wooed me. Who knew? That was the beauty of it. She could be anyone. The girl of my dreams who had been completely wowed by my "charisma," or a drunken slut who had felt she could do no better and decided to have her fun with me. No matter what, I would have a story for my friends. This wasn't so bad now that I gave it some thought.

I heard another snort, drawing my attention once again to the lady in my bed. She was just now flipping over to her right side, mumbling a little as she turned. My brain yelled out "Duck!", but my body couldn't respond in time and I remained fixed on my knees, helplessly staring at the stranger in front of me.

And then time elongated. A minute squeezed into a second as I gaped at the sight in front of me. An appealing face sporting a pair of full lips, a slight pointed nose, and two large eyes lay on my flower-print pillow a couple of feet away from me. The eyes were shut, but I already knew their color. They were blue, light blue eyes that shone brightly when their owner became excited. I was looking at the face of my boss Beth Garcia. And while you couldn't tell at first glance, she had about eight years on me. Thirty-two to my twenty-four. I was trying to digest the implications of this when she yawned and opened her eyes.

I could only imagine what this must have been like for her, waking up in a strange bed to find your subordinate from work gaping at you from a couple feet away. To her credit she only let her eyes widen a little in surprise. Then she jumped back about four feet and hit her head against my bedroom wall. I don't think I had ever seen anyone move that fast.

"Shit!" She groaned and leaned forward, holding her head. As if the hangover wasn't bad enough. I stayed frozen, preferring to let her get this morning off on the wrong foot.

"Stu?" Mission accomplished.

"Um, no, it's Sam." I suddenly felt shy.

"Sam," she repeated, staring at me as if I wasn't actually there. I could see her frantically seeking out the right words in her head, editing what would be her sentences to me for the rest of the morning. Meanwhile, the silence suffocated us both. Finally, her face straightened into resolute lines and she spoke, slowly at first, but gaining speed as she began to get comfortable with the sound of her own voice.

"Look Sam, I'm not exactly sure what happened last night…clearly some mistakes were made…but things like this happen, and I'm sure as mature adults we can get past it. I mean, this is certainly something best left out of the office, seeing as we are both professional, career-minded individuals who would hate to have anyone see us as anything but. Am I right?"

Speak for yourself. Beth was causing my headache to amplify. It was bad enough I had to deal with her at the office, now I felt like my own private sanctuary was being defiled. I wanted her out of my room and exiled back to whatever world she operated in.

"Yeah, sure. Whatever." I hoped the exhausted expression on my face would convey the message that I didn't give a shit but, still worried about any repercussions, Beth continued to talk.

"Look Sam, I'm sure last night was fun, but we both know better than to mix work and romance. I just want to make sure you understand how something like this, if it got out around the office, could reflect badly on both of us. Reflect reaaaaally badly. Do you understand where I'm coming from? I need to make sure we're on the same page."

Something in me snapped. All I wanted to do was scream and tell her I didn't care about her fucking career and her fucking ambition and her fucking professionalism. She meant nothing to me, and the only reason I wouldn't say anything at work was because I wouldn't want to be associated with *her*. But I restrained myself. Sort of.

"So does this mean you don't want to start the day off with a banana?" I asked, completely straight-faced. She looked confused, so I gestured towards my crotch. "I mean, last night you kept on begging for it, and I don't see why the fun can't continue. It's a new day, right? With new adventures?"

I wish I had my camera. Beth's face started off absolutely shocked, then appalled, then furious, then fearful. All in a span of two seconds.

"You're kidding, right, Sam? I did not do that last night! I admit I don't remember much of what happened, but I would never do that. Never." She had an infuriating habit of repeating herself, as if that somehow the second time around her message gained more weight.

"I am veeeeery in control most nights; I really don't understand how I could have let myself do something like this." She also tended to stretch her words out with great drama, savoring every syllable like it was a precious gem about to leave her lips. Man, why did it have to be her? At that moment the sheet she had been covering herself with slipped down, exposing her right breast. Oh, that's why.

"I really don't know what came over me, I really don't know," she continued, staring at the ceiling as if besieging the heavens for an answer. Meanwhile, my eyes continued to enjoy the largesse of her nipple. She must have felt my stare because she quickly jerked up the sheet again, giving me an exasperated look. "Okay, we'll just have to move on and treat this situation as a lesson to be learned from." She finished that line with a stern nod in my direction.

I had dealt with just about enough.

"No banana it is!" I proclaimed as I got up off the floor and left the bedroom to the sound of her indignation. Man I could really use some Coco Puffs right about now. Some Coco Puffs and maybe a beer to help shake off this hangover.

Strolling into the kitchen, I was quickly blinded by the light streaming in through the windows. I looked at the clock perched on the wall to reaffirm that it was in fact six a.m. And those blinds were closed last night, which meant that someone had just opened them. Finn. It had to be Finn. Only Finn would be up, despite the fact that he too didn't have to be in at work until nine. Fucking Finn. Hardworking, handsome Finn, soon to be heading off to whatever the most prestigious medical school was. Awake at the ass-crack of dawn to accomplish something. The kid loved accomplishing things.

I reached into the fridge and found a can of beer between the fruit smoothie Finn had made last night and the forty that Mack hadn't had the staying power to get to before he passed out. I drank it as quickly as I could, because despite how badass I might fancy myself, a beer at this hour was not the ideal I was shooting for. After getting a couple of good burps out I felt a little better and proceeded to pour myself a huge bowl of Coco Puffs. I always thought they looked like the little shits my rabbit used to drop in big piles in the corner of his cage, but I got over that phobia as soon as their sugary goodness hit my tongue for the first time.

Working my way into our living room I saw plenty of beer cans strayed about. Most of those were Mack's doing. Sooner or later Finn, I, or someone else close to Mack had to have a talk with the guy about his life. But for right now it was hilarious watching it unfold on a daily basis. As if to reiterate the humor, I heard a mighty fart echo from down the hall, followed by an "oh yeah!" and a brief respite from the snoring that provided each morning's ambient noise. Thank god I had my music, which I quickly started up when my laptop flipped open. Today my real breakfast was not the Coco Puffs, but rather Retro Savvy, this great new band I had discovered through a friend a few weeks ago. Since then, they had had the honor of powering me through my waking hours. Today would be no different.

"Yo, dude," Mack mumbled as he entered the room scratching his ass. "Why are you up? It's really early." I wasn't sure how I hadn't noticed the creak of the bedsprings as he removed his bulk from the mattress, but it was hard not be aware of his presence now as he released gas yet again. "Whatever, you can tell me later. I'm taking a piss." He tussled my hair affectionately and kept on walking towards the bathroom, leaving a lingering stench in his wake.

He was only wearing a pair of briefs. I don't know why it was that Mack, of all my friends, would be the only one who refused to wear pants around the house. I think it was because I must have done something horrific in another life. Maybe I was Genghis Khan or something. That would explain why I was faced with Mack's ample behind every day. I guess he was always big, even when we started school, but his living habits had not encouraged any revision of that bigness. I had tried to get him to wear some pants, but Finn never complained, so it was just my preference against Mack's, and Mack outweighed me by about fifty pounds.

How this kid graduated college was beyond me. I asked him about his final GPA once and he just pointed at the diploma hanging on the wall of his room as if to say, "It's real, isn't it? What else matters?" What I knew for sure was that he drank more in four years at school than I would have thought possible for any one man. It showed. He would always be big, but it was in his face that you could see the telltale signs of one who enjoyed himself a little too much too often. But he still had a boyish look to him, and his deep brown eyes and matching curls managed to still get some attention from the ladies we encountered. If only his winning smile wasn't often followed with a burp. But that's why we loved him.

The toilet flushed and I heard the bathroom door open. An instant later my bedroom door did the same, initiating a great interaction that I wish I had been bold enough to run around the corner to witness. But what I heard was enough.

"Oh hello there…I didn't see you. Good morning!"

"Who are you?"

"I'm Beth. I work with…Sam. Pleased to meet you!" I imagined her sticking her hand out.

"You two fuck last night?" Silence. Awesome, beautiful silence.

"I honestly don't know how to answer that question. I honestly doooon't know."

"Seems like a simple enough question. But whatever. Nice to meet you, Beth. I'm Francis." Francis was his first name, Mackenzie his middle. I loved when Mack called himself Francis. With the exception of this one girlfriend he had had for a while sophomore year, no one called him anything but Mack. And that girl reverted to calling him Mack when she realized he was anything but a Francis. Yet he insisted on always introducing himself as such. Maybe he thought it gave him a starting point of respectability he would otherwise be lacking.

"Whatever." The politeness had left her voice. "Where's Sam?"

"Muff dawg? He's over by his computer. Muffy, you rock!" Mack cheered as he trudged back off to his bed. "Now I see why you woke up early! Stud!"

Beth emerged from the kitchen. Wearing one of my T-shirts and a pair of my boxers. And not looking pleased.

"Where are my clothes?"

"You're looking pretty good right now. Why not head off to work like that? It is casual Friday. Make a statement." I tried to smile to take the edge off my words, but it died in its infancy. Not worth the effort.

"It's Thursday. And where are my clothes?" She gave me a look I'd seen before. A look she delivered when she wanted to put a coworker in their place. I wouldn't acknowledge it to her, but it was a disturbing look, hinting a little at the beast within. I quickly scanned the room looking for her clothes.

"Over there." I said, pointing at the couch where her business suit lay crumpled. She briskly walked over, gathered it up in her arms, and walked just as briskly into the bathroom. I shrugged. However she wanted to be, I wasn't going to have this wreck my day. My day was only going to be wrecked once I got into work. In the meantime, I was going to listen to my music and check Facebook.

I was old enough to remember a time before sites like Facebook had dominated the social scene. But to be stripped of them now would be a much more dramatic loss than I would like to admit, especially in the years since I had graduated. It was always assumed that once you and your friends left the warm cocoon of collegiate life you would all eventually lose touch. The Internet changed all that. Facebook and sites like it created a social web that you gladly became entangled in, leading you to believe that despite not seeing a friend in a couple of years you were still in the know. Through the lens of your computer you could observe as they posted new jobs, new relationships, and new photos, all of it giving an illusion of closeness even as they led a life without you in it.

But Facebook only gave you a superficial glance, a misleading impression that those old friends you once saw daily were just a click away. For a select few it served as an invaluable tool in the struggle to maintain long-distance camaraderie, but mostly it just provided a welcome reminder that your old classmates still existed and were currently leading lives similar to your own. Safely preserved online, they helped diminish the inevitable alienation that accompanied life after school. With Facebook I could be sure I would never be completely alone.

As I scrolled through recently updated profiles I saw something disconcerting. Another marriage. My buddy Chris, who I hadn't seen in over a year, was now engaged to his long-time girlfriend Audrey. They had both graduated with me from Fulton, and while it made perfect sense that after four years of dating they would decide to get married, I still felt a bit rattled. That was the fourth engagement in the last few months. I had already been to two weddings since graduating almost three years ago and, although they were fun, I had always left the celebration feeling like time was moving too fast.

"Jesus Christ," I uttered softly as I stared at the screen. I wondered if I would get an invitation.

"Talking to yourself?" I almost jumped out of my seat in shock, so intent had I been on the nuptials in front of me.

"Where have you been, dude?" I said as I spun around in my chair. Finn was standing a few feet behind me, a sweaty sheen making his perfect complexion glow even more. "I'm guessing running?"

"What gave it away?" he replied as he untied his shoes, bright yellow things that must in some way contribute the amazing land speeds he attained. "The shorts? The headband? The heavy breathing?"

Finn was hardly breathing at all, seemingly not at all winded by whatever he had just done. He took off the headband, letting his long blond locks spill over his face. Intent on medical school, I honestly think he could have succeeded at male modeling. Square jaw, piercing blue eyes, the kind of athletic build that had been guaranteed at birth with his genetics. I couldn't resist asking. "How far did you go today?"

"Well, I'm thinking I really have to pick it up for the marathon, so today was around a dozen miles." He said it so nonchalantly I knew he wasn't bragging. Maybe because he knew from our few runs together that half that distance would have done me in.

"I just saw on Facebook that Chris is getting married to Audrey." That earned a raised eyebrow.

"Really? I always thought she was a bitch, but I guess they have been together a few years. That's wild stuff. Who's next? Mack?" We laughed at the improbability of that ever happening, but in the back of my mind the idea itself seemed sinister. A married Mack would conceivably be a markedly different person than my old college friend, the one I could always count on to be a lovable mess. However, that would be one hell of a bachelor party. Finn walked over to my seat and crouched beside me. I gave him a curious look. What was his deal? A ghost of a smile crossed his face.

"Oh, by the way, I found something interesting outside. Maybe it's your doing?"

"Outside?" I looked at him, but beyond the faint grin he wasn't giving anything away. I got up and went to the door he had left ajar. Poking my head through, I looked left, then right, then straight down. In front of me lay black lace underwear and a matching bra. I quickly picked them up and walked down the hall towards the bathroom, ignoring Finn as his eyes followed my journey across the house.

"Beth, I have something you might need!" I called through the door.

"What is it?" I heard a muffled voice call back.

"You're going to have to open the door!"

"Fine." She sounded funny.

She opened the door just a bit and poked her head out. She had been crying. Despite having seen many people cry in my life, I was always caught off guard when it happened.

"I thought you would like these," I said softly as I handed over her delicates.

"Where were…oh, forget it. Thanks." She took them as closed the door, sniffing a little when she did.

I looked at the clock again. It was almost seven now. I had better start getting ready as well.

2

ESCAPE FROM THE APARTMENT

I ENTERED MY bedroom and immediately turned on my iPod, causing two beautiful speakers to begin streaming out sound. More music, specifically the latest incarnation of my "wake up" mix. It usually would be replacing my "go to sleep" mix from the night before, but I hadn't managed to remember to put in the sleep mix before I had passed out on the floor.

I had mixes for every facet of my life. Happy mixes, angry mixes, sad mixes, driving mixes, summer mixes, winter mixes, even a much-anticipated "sexy-time mix" I had been working on for a while. I was, more than anything else, looking for test subjects before I finally was satisfied with this special combination of smooth sounds. I had already played what I had thus far compiled for both Mack and Finn, with mixed results. Mack felt that a few beers did a better job of putting a girl in the mood than any mix ever would, but I wasn't looking to hook up with the type of girls he did. Finn had complimented it as it had played in the background during one of his intense MCAT studying sessions, but when informed of its purpose in seducing the opposite sex he had scoffed, saying that he didn't need to use music as a crutch to get a girl. I briefly considered asking Beth for her opinion, but after our interaction outside the bathroom I decided against it. One day it would get finished, and woe to the female who stumbled across its path.

Yellow dress shirt. Gray pants. Black socks. Black shoes. The outfit was complete for today, slightly different than yesterday. I refused to think too much about the clothes I chose for work, because whatever creative energy I had was not going to be spent mixing and matching linens. I'd rather have it fester inside until finally it exploded without, changing my life's landscape to something radically different from what I currently surveyed every day.

I left my bedroom and headed to the bathroom, hoping that Beth was done with her crying so I could brush my teeth. The door was open. I entered and smelled something refreshing: the scent of a woman. For a minute I almost forgot how much I couldn't stand her and wished I had been able to hold her before she had woken.

I didn't appreciate what I saw in the mirror. I was looking a little gaunt, but only in my unshaven face. My body was not reacting well to the alcohol-fueled beating I was giving it at regular intervals, and I knew my diet was something most English sailors three hundred years ago would have scowled at. I now had a bit of a belly, only exaggerated by the muscles I had lost in my upper body. And if I wasn't mistaken there were some white hairs coming in on the sides of my head, slowly replacing their brown predecessors. Premature, just like my dad. Son of a bitch. Twenty-four years old. The worst thing was most of it had happened in the past year. I didn't remember once looking at myself in the mirror while at school and feeling a vague sense of dread. What could halt this seemingly inevitable slide? My body's decline I could still fix, if I had the desire. But the crow's feet around my tired gray eyes? Only a reminder of the times I had smiled more.

I left the bathroom in a foul mood and quickly took in a sight that made it worse. Finn, still stretching, was making Beth's day. She looked much better now, all made up and wearing a blouse and dress pants. She was laughing at something my roomie had just said. Giggling was more like it. This meant, like so many other women, she had already found a place in her heart for our aspiring doctor. Because Finn wasn't funny. He was smooth and said things that could be seen as humorous, but he wasn't laugh-out-loud funny. Not that I cared. She sucked. A lot. All the more reason to usher her out of the house as soon as possible.

"Hey Beth, you ready to head?" I felt like I had instantly killed the mood. Good. My half-hearted smile fizzled quickly on my face and I gestured to the door. They both turned to me, Finn in the middle of some absurd stretch where his head rested underneath the bend of his knee. Beth's eyes lost their laughter, but she still managed to keep her smile planted on her face.

"Oh, yes, sure. I was just getting to know your roommate Finn. Did you know my cousin went to Fulton as well? Where did you go again?"

"Fulton. I graduated with Finn a few years ago."

"Oh, you too? I bet you have some great stories! Were you two in fraternities? I was in a sorority."

"No, there wasn't a Greek scene at Fulton," I replied, trying to hide the distaste I felt. "But yeah, we had some times. For the best stuff you'd have to talk to Mack…I mean Francis. That is, if he can remember half of what he did."

"Look at Muff, so modest," Finn chided. "What Mack accomplished was heavy-handed. Muffy had creative flair. Like the ski helmet bong? Oh man, that was genius."

"Why do you call him Muff?" Beth asked him, as if I wouldn't be the one to pose that question to. Goddamnit, I was the one who had sex with her, and the way she was acting towards Finn you half expected them to be sharing a post-coital cigarette.

"I actually don't even remember anymore. Do you remember how you got it, Muff?"

"I remember how I got it and I remember who gave it to me. And so should you." Fuck man, had he really forgotten or was his brain low on blood from the run?

Finn frowned, looking wounded. "Yeah dude, I remember who gave it to you. We all remember. It's a good nickname." He gave Beth a sideways look and got up off the floor. "Nice meeting you, Beth. I gotta go shower now. The lab rats might not mind the smell, but you never know about my coworkers." He walked by me and clapped me on my shoulder as he did, whispering "The Muffin Man!" in my ear. Then the bathroom door was closed, leaving me with memories and a bitch in my living room.

Beth looked at me quizzically but didn't say anything. For once I was thankful for her veneer of politeness.

"You ready?" I asked.

"Sounds good to me!" The fake enthusiasm was nauseating.

We walked down the hall towards the door and passed an empty room on the right, its vacancy amplifying the silence of the early morning. I hadn't looked in there in what seemed like forever and was furious when she made a point of stopping at its entryway.

"Did one of your roommates move out?" She peered in, seeing the only thing that could be seen. A sign, hanging from a nail above an otherwise unadorned wall in an empty room. A sign stolen from a strip club that said: "Pete's Palace: The Gentleman's Club for Royalty." Despite not having acknowledged the room in ages, I knew that sign would still be there. "He couldn't handle you three wild men, could he?"

"No, he was the wildest of all of us. So wild that he killed himself." There. That should shut her up. Now get in the car and don't make me remember things that should be forgotten.

She looked at me in amazement as I opened the front door for her and impatiently indicated she should exit. "Are you serious?"

"Yes I'm serious, now let's go!" She went, and I followed. Walked to the car, started it, and left the apartment. An apartment that I knew I couldn't handle for the rest of the day now that she had brought up Pete. For once that fluorescently lit cubicle would be my escape, protecting me from my forever-departed friend.

3

THE LIFE AND TIMES OF PETER HOLLIS

THE COMMUTE WAS uneventful. I had started to drive in the direction of our office before Beth made a noise in her throat. I looked over at her, hoping that sound didn't mean what I thought it meant. She smiled girlishly and asked if I could possibly bring her back home to her house in the North End so she could freshen up a bit. This way, she said, I wouldn't have to worry about driving her up and we could save ourselves the embarrassment of entering the office together. What she meant, of course, was save *herself* the embarrassment, but I obliged her anyway. I couldn't stand being near her any longer. A half hour later I pulled my car up in front of a nice brick place and said goodbye, her response being that she hoped we could keep all this between the two of us. I nodded through clenched teeth and sped away.

The moment I began to head back towards the direction of the office I hit major traffic. Worse than even I could have imagined. Must have been an accident. That thought led to a familiar battle with my better half, because no matter how much I tried I couldn't restrain the brief unadulterated thrill of excitement that came with the thought of witnessing a wreck. It wasn't the thought of death that got my blood going, but rather the sight of something dramatic in my mundane existence. I wouldn't have been surprised if every one of the other motorists was enduring the same minor crisis of conscience. Mothers might tell their children, "Oh dear, I hope they made it out alright!", and that would be true. What they neglected to mention to their offspring was the other thought that popped into their head at the same time. This thought, roughly summed up, said: "Man, the traffic is *really* backed up. I sure hope they haven't taken the wrecks away yet. Maybe it was one of those ten-car pileups! Haven't seen one of those in a while!"

And there was nothing wrong with that. The same thing could be applied to sex. Don't try to pretend you didn't get a thrill when you saw that sixteen-year-old sway by in her short skirt. That doesn't mean you should hit on her, or try to cause accidents just to see the Hummer nail the Mini-Cooper. But be honest with yourself about those visceral feelings that rise up in you before your brain can grasp how undeniably inappropriate they are. The redeeming thing isn't that you don't have a deep-seated desire to see something magnificently destructive, but that you can still summon up the empathy for those who were unfortunate enough to get caught up in that accident. You know if it had been someone else in their car that victim would be have been looking on thinking: "Man, I didn't think my Camry could stay on two wheels for that long! Sick!"

One thing was clear: I was going to be in traffic for a long time. And no matter how loud I turned up my "stave off the going-to-work depression" mix, there would be no avoiding the thoughts churning in the back of my head about Pete. That motherfucking piece of shit Pete.

*****

Pete was the glue. Whatever else came to your mind when you thought of Pete, you first had to acknowledge that fact. No matter what group of people he found himself in, he made their bonds tighter. He elevated their energy and had them creating memories even when it appeared everyone was ready to turn in. He was the ideal college kid, the guy who everyone on campus knew and who you considered it a privilege to have as a friend. Always funny, always there when anyone needed someone to be there, he amazed me at how he managed to be so many things to so many people. And I got to be his roommate the last two years at Fulton. The two best years of my life.

We were similar in a lot of ways, but he was me writ large. We played off each other, but his jokes were always a little funnier. Not that I minded. I laughed harder than anyone else.

Pete had a face different from many of the well-bred sons and daughters who attended Fulton. He didn't have a strong jaw or a proud nose. His eyes were green, but a pale unimpressive green. Moreover, he had a famous snaggletooth, noteworthy simply because he existed in a realm where everyone had perfectly straight teeth. And if they didn't by the time they came to Fulton, their parents wouldn't hesitate to slap a pair of three-thousand-dollar braces on their son or daughter. My parents had identified me at a young age as a dreaded "tongue thruster," one whose sinful habits must be curbed as soon as possible before it damaged his life irrevocably. After years of retainers, strategically placed spikes on the back of my bottom front teeth, and finally braces, I was prepared for a life at Fulton. Pete's parents lacked the money for such extravagance, so he had a snaggletooth. Somehow, once he arrived at Fulton his snaggletooth became a sexy calling card. Only Pete.

His female foil was Nora Williamson, who he dated from second semester of freshman year onward. During this time, despite it being a well-known fact he was with her, it was made amply clear by many girls that they were interested. It was his magnetism. He drew them like moths to the flame. Time after time they were rebuked, but even with their wounded pride they would still subtly pursue.

Not that Nora cared. If there was one person I had ever met who could match Pete's strength of character, it was her. It wouldn't have surprised me if the only reason he refused their advances was because he knew she was simply *better* than any other girl on campus. While not gorgeous, she had more of a subdued appeal, her long blond hair softly surrounding a heart-shaped face. Athletic, she moved with a quiet grace that you appreciated even more once you knew her; it was a manifestation of her spirit. When Pete initially pointed her out to me across the campus I was relatively unfazed, but the first time I interacted with her I couldn't have been more impressed. She was a girl who, the instant she smiled, made everyone feel like they had just done something special. It was a benevolent smile which spoke of a truly beautiful person. When that smile faded, the memory of it lived on, casting a revealing light on everything else about her. Its kindness was felt in her words, its sex appeal present in her easygoing confidence, its good humor evident in her jokes.

Never, with Pete or Nora, was there ever a question of one being too good for the other. They counterbalanced each other perfectly. I don't know if I could claim to have the same sort of sublime connection with Kate, my girlfriend at the time, but it never crossed my mind to compare. Kate was the first love of my life and, as such, she was greater than even Nora. She was also good friends with Nora, and memories of the four of us hanging out on the quad together still burned brightly in my mind years later.

Pete's crowning moments came both in private and in public, because his public image was inseparable from his private self. An illustration of one such moment was one night sophomore year at our friend Tom's cabin. We were all playing beer pong and, although Pete was no pro, he soon found himself in a groove. He and his partner claimed victory ten straight times, after which he stumbled outside and vomited in the bushes. When I discovered him on his knees he paused long enough to give me a thumbs up, and ten minutes later he had rejoined the party.

Later on at the same party, a situation arose in which Nate, a senior rugby player who was a friend of Tom's, announced his plan to exit the party and drive back an hour to campus. The problem with this was that he had been Pete's beer pong partner and was thus incredibly hammered. Silence greeted his proclamation. No one planned on riding back with someone who might not even remember the drive. Multiple kids, including myself, approached Nate and told him it was a horrible idea and that he should give us his keys.

"No, you guys, I'm fine, I really am," he said, patting us on our shoulders reassuringly while using our bodies to steady his own.

Tom took Nate's hand off his shoulder. "Dude, think about it. You've had way too much. It's retarded. You'll end up wrapped around a tree." He held out his hand. "Give me your keys."

"Nope. Fuck you man, I'm fine." Nate had a reputation as an angry drunk and he pushed off of us as he headed to the door. This left us two options: call the cops on our friend or let him go. We chose the latter. Pete chose a third option. Before Nate made it to the door Pete intercepted him.

"Hey bud, what's up? Heading home?" He made sure to stand in front of the door as he asked these questions.

"Pete! S'up, man. We had a great night tonight right? Ten in a row!" Nate slurred.

"Yeah, and I carried you the whole time. But hey, that's fine, you're probably still sore from today's match."

"What?! Bullshit! I carried you, man. I made all the clutch shots."

"Well then, how about you and me, one on one? Best out of three. We'll see who's really the better player."

Nate shook his head. "Sorry man, I'm done drinking. I'm going to head back to Fulton. There's a female waiting for me on campus."

Pete looked at Nate for a long second, then nodded his head in agreement. "Fine dude, but can you do me one favor? Nora wanted to play one game with you the whole night and I was hogging you. Do you think you could play one game with her and she'll drink for both of you? Mack and Muff will play against you two. One game with Nora, Nate, that's all I'm asking." He gestured to where his girlfriend stood talking to a couple of friends. When she saw Nate looking at her Nora's face broke out in a big smile and she made a throwing motion with her hand.

Nate sighed. "Fine, one game." He swung his head around a couple of times before he realized both Mack and I were on either side of him. "Let's go, guys."

"Great! I'm just going to go take a piss outside. You better hope Nora's as good as me or else you're in deep shit," Pete taunted as he exited the front door.

The game went into overtime, and despite what Nate had said about not wanting to drink anymore, he refused to let Nora drink for him. Pete was outside for a long time taking his piss, but came back in just in time to see Nate sink the winning shot.

"Wooooo!" Nate hollered as he high-fived Nora and pumped his fist. "See that, Pete! Still a winner!"

Pete laughed and shook his hand. "Nice, man, now you want to stick around and sober up a bit?"

Still smiling, Nate shook his head no. "Nope, I can still get back into campus by midnight. Later, guys!" He stumbled to the door, but as people made to intercept him Pete waved them off. He didn't look the slightest bit worried. A minute later we found out why.

Outside, Nate swore loudly. We heard him running back towards the house and the door flew open.

"What the fuck!" he yelled, looking around the room. "Not funny, guys. Really not funny. Who did it?!" He looked furiously around the room at every bewildered person there. I had no idea what he was talking about, but I wasn't altogether surprised to see Pete raising his hand.

"It was me, Nate. I did it. No worries, you'll get it back in the morning."

Nate's eyes widened a little in surprise as he regarded Pete, but they quickly regained most of their dangerous glint.

"No, Pete, you'll give it back now. I'm not joking, man. Give it back." He slowly advanced across the now tense room, a very well-built kid approaching one who was not. Pete didn't flinch.

"No way. You're in no shape to drive, and I'm not letting you kill someone else or yourself."

Nate was in front of Pete now, fists clenched. They stood about a foot apart, neither showing any signs of backing down. Everyone was completely silent, anticipating the worst. It was Nate who cracked first. He roared, spun away from Pete and walked back outside, slamming the door behind him. We waited a couple of seconds, then followed.

He was sitting in the driver's side of his SUV, gripping the steering wheel and staring straight ahead. The car wasn't started. I guessed this was largely due to the fact that his front right tire was missing.

A couple of suppressed laughs could be heard as the partygoers made their way back inside. Pete was lounging on the couch, drinking a beer.

"Like I said, he'll get it back in the morning."

Pete was true to his word. When Nate woke up in his car the next morning his wheel was back on. That next summer he would get arrested for DUI. When he heard, Pete just shrugged his shoulders. That night we choked when presented with the opportunity to possibly prevent a tragedy. With Pete, and this was true from the moment I first met him, there never seemed to be hesitation. He always realized what should be done and he did it, inspiring with the most casual of demeanors.

The story at Tom's cabin was well known. There were many other things Pete did during his time at Fulton that were known to few but just as noteworthy. A working-class kid at a school riddled with trust funds, he still scrounged up five hundred dollars and drove five hours to bail an old friend from high school out of jail. That in itself was something unusual for any self-absorbed collegian focused on finals or getting drunk. What made it something unique was that it was the one-year anniversary of his and Nora's storybook romance. He was gone from eight a.m. until midnight that Sunday, skipping out on their special day without a moment's notice. Nora was a cool, understanding girl, but she was still mildly infuriated that he would be out of the state for a day they had been planning for a month. He knew he would be in trouble when he returned, but he still took the trip. According to him, he was all his buddy had (although to my knowledge he hadn't talked to him since high school) and it wasn't an option for him to ditch him.

Peter Hollis was viewed as something exceptional. He was one of the untouchables, a person who few could find any fault with. Except his parents. Maybe it was because they had little respect for what a school like Fulton could deliver to its students, or because on the surface Pete's grades were less than stellar. He once told me that in high school he had been one of the top students in his class, but all the effort he put into acing his classes was just so he could get into a school like Fulton. Once in college, it was about the lectures, not the homework. He loved his courses and his consistent Cs did not do justice to the often brilliant points he would bring up in class discussion or the burning passion he had for philosophy. There was one time when the sole reason he was absent at our Hegel seminar was because he had gotten involved in a riveting debate with the professor who had just exited the classroom our lecture was being be held in. I left class to see him bidding the impressed academic farewell. He then turned to me and said "Man, Professor Tracy really has some interesting points on Hume. We should definitely take his class next semester." His parents weren't aware of these things, but were they to know they still would have found Pete to be a bit of a disappointment. They loved him, as good parents should, and couldn't help but crack grins when he was in his element, but I think they always had higher goals for their one and only son, something more worthwhile than being one of the most potent personalities to ever grace Fulton's campus. He knew this and I think it bothered him a little, but he once explained to me how he rationalized it.

"Muff, if I followed my parents' dreams and lived the life they want for me, I doubt I would have enough time after I retired to still live the life I want for me. Wanna toss a disc?"

The one thing that could have been Pete's downfall was, in fact, Pete's downfall. He couldn't decide what life, other than the college one, he wanted to live. His toast at the raucous "night before graduation" party summed it up perfectly.

"Gentleman! Ladies!" he called out to the wildly drunk class of 2005. The astonishing thing was how quickly the noise level of the five hundred kids assembled dropped to a whisper. Five hundred pairs of eyes all did their best to focus on the shaggy-haired skinny kid with the backwards hat standing atop a keg. I never understood why Pete didn't join the debate club. His power as an orator was unrivaled. But even if he had been a horrible public speaker, everyone gathered there would have still wanted him to say something. They all knew him, and they all loved him. I still remember every word he spoke, for although he lived for almost two years past that night it may as well have been his swan song. The peak of a great man's life, a peak thankfully ingrained upon the souls of five hundred other malleable youths.

While he didn't have an impressive figure, Pete did have passion to spare. He seemed to vibrate when he became excited, showcasing a spirit that captivated those exposed. More than ever this was true that night.

"Hey everyone, it's me, Pete!" he said, swaying a little as he extended his beer in one hand.

"Hey Pete!" everyone yelled back in unison. Somebody in the back slurred something loudly about wanting to bear his child.

"Okay, so this is it," he began, making eye contact with everyone at once. Ask anyone there and they would tell you he gave them in particular a special glance. "Tonight and tomorrow morning will be the last time all of us will be together in one place. After that we go to the four winds, and even with the wonders of the Internet and cell phones, many of us might never see or talk to each other again." Tears were already forming in many eyes in the crowd. "But I want you all to know where you can find me: 14 Pine Street, Natick, Massachusetts, the basement. And you have to address it to the basement or I guarantee my parents will read whatever you send me." Laughter echoed around the quad.

"Seriously though, I am going to miss you all so much. Well, except for Finn. That kid honestly is a huge dick. Oh, Finn, you're here? Good to see you buddy! You hear me talking about how well-endowed you are?! Anyways, I wanted to let you all know that while you're all going to occupy some part of me when I leave, it's just going to be a shadow of what you're giving me right now. College for me has been all I could have asked for and more, and I hope Fulton has given you all something special to remember. Whether it was…" He paused to mentally unearth some suitable examples.

"Whether it was Mack taking a dump on Dean O'Reilly's lawn… yes, I see you Mack, just try to make it through the night alive. I just hope some freshman lady will take pity on you these your last hours in college and finally make a man out of you." Pete stopped again, looking to the sky while he collected his thoughts. "Where was I? Yes, whether it's Mack doing what he does best, or Christine making out with the lead singer of whatever band was lucky enough to be playing here each year, or Paul actually giving us a reason to root for men's squash, the memories I made at Fulton will last me a lifetime. And they better, because I highly doubt we'll ever be allowed to do what we did here ever again." There was a brief silence as the soon-to-be grads pondered this.

"But don't worry about that. What can't be duplicated is all the more special because of the fact that it can only be done once. So use your last hours as an undergrad to celebrate. This is a night where extremes are allowed. You can't get drunk enough, you can't be too cheesy, and most of all you can't get turned down by the opposite sex. The vibe here, right now, is something I'm going to treasure." He stopped and appeared mildly ill, as though he had gorged too heavily on the nostalgia. Blinking, he straightened his posture and delivered the rest of his address.

"If the rest of my life is shit, I'll always have this. I love you all. Especially Nora and my boy Muffy! Fulton! Colleeeeeeege!"

He stepped down from the keg only to be hoisted up by Mack onto his broad shoulders. What followed was literally ripped out of some cliched Hollywood ending, but it resonated more than I ever would have thought possible. A chant of "Pete" started, beginning with Mack's deep baritone and spreading throughout the crowd. "Pete!" the kids repeated with reverence, as if he was everything good about existence. The chanting lasted half a minute until Pete got a Mack chant going, which lasted about five seconds. Then everyone went back to drinking.

Everyone wanted to see all their fellow grads that night, and I was pretty sure that over the duration of the party I managed to share a moment with all my close friends. Almost all the encounters blended together, drunken and overflowing with emotion. However, one instant in particular stood out.

Before Pete gave his speech, when the party was still filling up, he, Nora, Kate, and I all sat under an old oak in the quad. We were a fair distance away from the party as it increased in sound and volume, allowing us the freedom to hear what each other said. We didn't say much.

Nora leaned up against Pete while Kate and I held hands in silence. All of us smiled, at each other and at the night in general.

"So, this isn't so bad is it?" Pete asked the group.

We all shook our heads no. Nora leaned over and kissed her boyfriend, and I think I heard her whisper "I love you" into his ear. Or at least that's what I assumed, because he mouthed "I love you too" back to her. A rare show of semi-public affection between the two of them, and it seemed fitting. I squeezed Kate's hand a little tighter and she did the same to mine. We all sat there, saying nothing, breathing in the air of the late spring night and feeling immortal.

I had never been so grateful to be alive.

*****

The next day one person was conspicuously absent from graduation. Where Pete went no one knew, including Nora and his parents. I finally found him when I was moving the last of my stuff from our room. Or rather, he found me. My parents and younger sister were outside trying to fit my couch on top of our Subaru Forrester. The fact that it was a six-hour ride did not seem to faze my dad, who had given me this couch four years earlier and who repeatedly said he would be damned if he wasn't bringing it back home safe and sound.

"Where the fuck have you been, dude?!" I demanded the second Pete popped his head into the room. "Was your plan to miss graduation all along?"

He gave me a long look and let the rest of his body enter the room. He was still wearing his clothes from last night, and he definitely still smelled like last night. I did not like what I was seeing, and the look he was giving me was making me profoundly uneasy.

I repeated my earlier question, this time with a tremor of fear in my voice. Pete's attention was riveted to the floor for a long time, and when he looked up I finally identified the nature of that look he was giving me. It was guilt. But more than just guilt.

"Look, man, if it's about graduation I'm sure your parents will forgive you. I mean, you can always point out you actually did graduate, and I'm pretty sure that's more than Mack did."

Pete still didn't respond and slowly let his lanky frame fall to the ground. He sat there for a solid minute in silence, cross-legged on the bare floor, and I waited. Finally, he looked up at me and tears were in his eyes. It was the only time I had ever see him cry in the four years we had known each other. Through the tears his gaze pinned me down, overwhelming me.

"Muff, I cheated on Nora last night. I had sex with this random freshman girl and woke up in her dorm this morning. I just told Nora what happened. She told me it's over." He paused for a second, and seeing me desperately trying to digest what he had just said, he waved his hand in my direction, as if to forestall any response I might have. "I've been thinking all day about what possessed me to do it, and I think I finally figured out why. It's not Nora, who's perfect as far as I'm concerned, and it wasn't the first-year, whose name I don't even remember." He blinked a couple of times and sniffed a little.

"After I gave that speech last night, something in me cracked. I should have seen it coming. I've blinded myself the last four years, pretending that everything would be fine when I graduated, but the truth is I don't think it will be. Fuck man, I don't want it to end. We've had too much fun for it to end! I don't want to move on, and I don't want to lose what I have here." He let his burning gaze drop from my own to the floor.

"So I grabbed the youngest, hottest girl I could find and I fucked her. I slept with her so, for at least one night, I could imagine that I had three more years left here. And you know what? It almost worked. I woke up in Howard House sleeping with this girl and her freshman roomie above me, and for about ten seconds I thought I was a freshman again."

He paused and gave me another dose of this new angst-ridden stare of his. "That's the problem with all this," he said, gesturing to our now-empty room. "It's a goddamn mind-fuck. You're supposed to immerse yourself in it, but when you leave it's like exiting the womb. Except this time we won't have our parents to watch over us."

I remember feeling terrified. Not that Pete had had this moral and existential breakdown, but that it all made sense in a Darwinian way. The creature perfectly adapted to one environment often does not possess the ability to survive in a drastically different clime. It hit me then that Pete never talked about life post-college. A lot of us suffered from cognitive dissonance regarding the inevitability of this post-adolescent window closing, but Pete refused to even discuss what his plans were. We had just assumed he would do something noteworthy, like he had during every minute of his time at Fulton. Apparently he had thought that too, until reality bit. Hard. I was just glad I was the only one to see the idol fall from grace. Better for just me to have his legendary speech undermined by this meltdown than all the other bright-eyed post-grads heading out to make their mark, buoyed by the words of their eminent visionary. I would hate for them to feel the same nausea I was currently experiencing.

I walked over to where he lay and seated myself. I tossed an arm around him with a certainty I didn't feel and spoke kind words of comfort.

"Pete, shut your bitch mouth. Everything is going to work out. Leaving college is a challenge for you to outdo yourself. And I'm pumped to see how you manage to do that."

He turned to me, half believing. "Fuck, you're right, Muff. Things will figure themselves out. And me and Nora would have been in trouble anyway right? I mean, she's off to grad school at Oxford, and long-distance won't work for that long. Better to do something reprehensible now and make a clean break."

"You don't mean that."

"No, I don't. I can't believe I even said that. I fucked up so royally here. I don't blame her. On graduation day? I'm lucky she didn't take my balls as souvenirs of her time here." A moment of quiet ensued, followed by Pete pulling himself off the floor as he grinned ruefully. I knew he was only smiling for my benefit, and that made it worse. "Anyways! Time to make amends with the parents. I would hate to have them be disappointed in me." The sarcasm was sharp and sudden, but not surprising. He extended his hand and pulled me up as well. I didn't know what to say, but looking at him I knew he understood.

"Stay in touch, buddy. Still sure about Boston?"

"As sure as anything at this point in my life," I replied.

"Exactly. That's what makes these the most exciting time of our lives. Or so we're told."

"So we're told." I quietly repeated, not really believing but pretending to for Pete's sake.

"Yep. Alright, bring it in buddy." We hugged for one long second before he broke the embrace and headed to the door.

"And what about you? Still bound for the parents' basement?!"

He stopped halfway out of the room and spun on his heels, looking into the distance thoughtfully. "Nah, change of plans. I'm thinking going out West is a better idea. I'll let you know when I find a spot worth settling down and raising a family in. Until then, tell your parents I say hey and pass along my number to your sister. Haven't seen her in a little while. She's turning into quite the young lady!"

He waved and walked out. I wouldn't see him for a year.

4

WELCOME TO THE WORKPLACE

I WAS ALWAYS on the verge of the unconscious. Sleep deprivation was an accepted part of my week, the constant companion that fuzzed out my waking moments. It surrounded me in a haze I could never really escape from, and it was caused almost entirely by my unwillingness to adjust to my early working hours. I still, three years later, went to bed at the same times I did in college. Around two a.m. every morning I would give up on the previous day and accept the necessity of sleep. Waking up the next morning at seven, I was left with just enough rest to function, but not nearly enough to function well. I envied the people that could survive on next to no sleep, those who scorned the sleeping patterns of the common people. But I knew if I could make it on three hours of sleep I would only sleep two.

This was because my dismissal of sleep wasn't rooted in a disdain for it, but rather a refusal to embrace the next day of my life. The instant after I fell asleep I would be awake and catapulted into tomorrow. I much preferred to enjoy the early morning hours as a free man than as a sleeping man. Strangely enough, it was those hours from midnight until two (assuming I wasn't drunk) that I felt the most alert. After an entire day of fighting off sleep, it was only at the end that I claimed victory. A victory I had to surrender when I passed out again. It was a vicious cycle that I broke every weekend, only to immediately restart Sunday night.

Now, after forty-five minutes in traffic, the effects of the minimal slumber I had gotten the night before were being felt.

A honk snapped my head off my steering wheel. I felt briefly disoriented before I realized I was on my way to work. Traffic had moved forward, and I hadn't moved with it. There was now a clear pathway to my exit, but as I maneuvered over a black BMW (why was it always a BMW?) swerved from two lanes over to make the same move. It narrowly avoided clipping the front of my car and, as I hit the brakes, the cars behind me honked again. I honked and my hand, middle finger prominent, extended from my window. I saw the driver's hand emerge and do the same. We both took the same exit, my car directly behind his. A pair of right turns later we were both in the company parking lot, and I watched in disbelief as the Beamer pulled into Legacy Communications' Executive Vice-President parking space. I brought my car to a halt at a spot about fifty feet away and sat frozen. A half minute passed before a well dressed silver-haired gentleman exited his car and, after giving my own vehicle a long look, continued to the entrance of the building. I could only hope he didn't recognize me, that he was too concerned with grand company affairs to worry himself with an entry-level drone.

It was now nine fifteen, and unlike my superior I couldn't afford to be much later to work. But I still waited for the current song by Retro Savvy to finish before I unplugged my iPod and tossed on my headphones. It gave me the slightest excuse to extend my time in my car before I ponderously made my way over to the office. When I finally arrived at the revolving door I paused, staring into the lobby. It seemed to be infinitely dimmer in there compared to the outside world I currently inhabited. Where I was, it was spring. The smell of spring, especially in New England, was an odor that always felt so crisp, so right. It was the scent of renewal, signifying yet another triumph over the quiet death of winter. The snow was almost gone, and in its place patches of green were emerging. Soon the trees would have all their leaves back, and I could almost see their branches shiver with anticipation. In the distance those trees seemed infinitely more impressive than the towering building I was about to enter. When I left this office nine hours later they would still be there, having enjoyed natural light and the tantalizingly temperate breeze that was presently blowing through my hair. I would look up at them, knowing I had just sacrificed another day doing something that delivered absolutely nothing of value to my life besides income. With that thought, I took my headphones out, pushed my way through the door, and walked towards the elevator. I caught it just as its doors were closing.

"Hey Sam, how's it going?" was the greeting I received the instant I entered. Normally I would quickly respond with one of three prepared responses. They were:

"Doing just fine! How about you?"

"You know, same old same old. You?"

Grunt. "Okay."

The last of these replies was reserved for my exceptionally hung-over days, when speaking more than a few words for the first couple of hours was asking far too much. But none of these would suit Lucie, the poser of this particular question. Income wasn't the only reason I reported for work day after day.

She was cute in the way that made you instinctively want to kiss her. Short, curly red hair and a smattering of freckles around a button nose, sparkling green eyes, and the perpetual half smile of a girl who always seemed to be in on some inside joke. I wanted to be in on that joke. She was tiny, just over 5 feet, but managed to emit a womanly air that guaranteed she would only be carded at a club because the bouncer wanted a couple extra seconds to soak her in. That mature vibe intimidated me, made me tongue-tied where I usually could maintain at least a semblance of cool. The string of social stumbles around her would only continue today, but to an extent even I couldn't have predicted possible.

She looked at me, smiling that half-smile. "Sam, you there, buddy?" She waved her hand in front of my face and I immediately responded.

"Yeah, sorry, I'm kinda out of sorts because tomorrow is the one-year anniversary of my best friend's suicide and I've been thinking a lot about it."

I couldn't even comprehend how those words left my mouth. If I knew one thing about the corporate environment it was that you kept serious personal stuff personal. To confess my own troubled state of mind to any colleague would invite plenty of awkwardness, but to open up to

Lucie in the elevator first thing in the morning?! Immediately feeling a flush steal up my neck, I quickly broke eye contact and stared fascinated at the elevator buttons.

There was an agonizing silence of a few seconds before I felt her hand on my own. She squeezed it lightly and let go, saying, "That sucks so much. Let me know if there is anything I can do." I turned and stole an embarrassed glance, expecting to see some sort of feigned awkward pity. There was none.

Her emerald eyes were deep pools of empathy. Real empathy…and something else? Before I could consider things further, the doors opened at the twentieth floor.

"Thanks," was all I managed before she beckoned for me to lead the way out. I did, and as we went to our opposite ends of the office she gave me a quick wave accompanied by that same sincere look of concern. I tried to comprehend that I might have, after two and a half years of working here, finally managed to make progress with my crush, but my thoughts fragmented as I rounded the corner and bumped into the driver of the Beamer. I quickly muttered an "Excuse me" and cast my eyes low as I walked by. He did the same, but in some dark recess of his brain he made the connection I feared. I heard his footsteps stop and felt his eyes bore into my back.

As I took a right and out of his line of sight, I heard the following exchange:

"Hey, Donald, how's the golf game?"

"Hey there, Todd. Same old, same old. It's going to give me a heart attack if my kids don't first! Say, Todd, do you know that scruffy-looking tall kid who just walked by?"

"Tall kid? Scruffy? A new intern?"

"No, I think he's been here for a while…"

Donald's voice thankfully trailed off. I would rather not know if I was a marked man.

Making a beeline for my cubicle, I rudely woke my computer from its sleep and tossed on my headphones. As the sound flowed through my head I immediately felt relief. My life was oases of musical bliss divided by wide expanses of barren tundra. Whether I was in my house, my car, or my cubicle, any alone time I had was enhanced as a result of the music humming in the background. Some people might find it a distraction, but any tangent a song brought me on was a welcome one.

One day, a few months into my stay at Legacy, I realized with mild annoyance that I forgotten my headphones. Over a few hours' time that irritation slowly morphed into something more sinister. I became acutely aware of my surroundings, of the jarring mechanical office noises and infuriating voices of my coworkers. My frown evolved into a leg twitch and a clenched jaw, then a tightness in my chest. By the end of the day I had a very real desire to bite something, to feel flesh give way to the tear of my incisors. Only then did I realize how much of my mental stability was predicated on the distance I felt from the world around me.

I wasn't the only one. About six months ago a coworker I really bonded with named Frank had uttered the quote that summed up why he tossed the headphones in.

"I can't hear anything with these in. Which, now that I think of it, is exactly why I put them in," he had told me, and I had laughed at the truth of it.

He was fired not too long afterwards. Wasn't meeting the company standards of excellence or something.

It would make sense for Frank's corporate demise to scare me straight and push me to greater efficiency, but it didn't. I counted on something else entirely: anonymity. I stayed under the radar in a very large corporation and didn't fuck up whatever tasks were assigned to me. And I was fine. People had to notice you to demand more of you. Unfortunately for Frank, he was black. This meant, in a company lacking any racial diversity, he never stood a chance being himself. I could imagine the conversations that took place regarding Frank's work.

"You see that email Frank had sent out earlier this week?"

"Frank?"

"The black guy who sits in the corner"

"Oh, Frank! Yeah I know him. And I did see that email. Clear lack of effort there."

The big issue at hand was Donald. Donald had noticed me, and in the worst way possible. Would he decide to bring scrutiny to my work

I couldn't afford to have? Only time would tell. The truth was, I really didn't give a shit. It would be a hassle finding a new job, but they were out there. That was the beauty of not having your job define your life. Or having anything define your life.

5

DELVING INTO THE DOLDRUMS

A DAY IN a corporate office for me could be compared to the life of a lazy, resentful farmer who is struggling because of a drought but realizes with any rain comes more farming. I suffered, but I suffered knowing that at least I didn't have to actively engage in something I hated. Like the bitter farmer, I could sit back and waste my life as I saw fit. And as long as I didn't get promoted the drought would remain. The fact that I feared a promotion marked a drastic psychological change. I now actively sought mediocrity in order to possess a minimum of stress. But there was a price to be paid for this refusal of success: the knowledge that I was not going to be receiving praise any time soon. No one was proud of me, least of all myself. I was a survivor, not an achiever.

Not being actively engrossed in my work meant the day passed excruciatingly slowly. The only highlight this particular morning was Beth's email to our team at ten o'clock explaining how, due to a stomach bug, she would be working remotely from her apartment today. Maybe her hangover was worse than I had initially thought. After that brief respite the daily routine once again reigned supreme: emails, phone calls, chats via instant messenger, and occasionally staring off into space for minutes on end. I often wondered if I would ever get any work done if I had a view of the outside world from my desk.

Thankfully, there were a few conference calls to add variety to the day. I worked on multiple client teams, each dealing with different corporate contacts with varying personalities. Yet somehow, these calls all seemed to play out the same way. Exchange of pleasantries, followed by a recap of the week's activities, and then a long discussion about the direction the client wished to go in. The clients would drone on as they had the previous week, and my managers would roll their eyes, proceeding to chime in with chipper affirmatives.

It doesn't sound enthralling. And it wasn't. But it was a great chance for me to catch up on my sleep. I might not want to sleep during the night, but I considered any time I was unconscious at work to be a blessing. During my first few months at the company I had gone through three stages of thought regarding these hour-long meetings. The first stage consisted of a constant state of alertness for any client demands that might directly impact me. The fear was that I would space out and snap back to attention just in time to hear: "So you'll have that done by end of day, Sam?" That blind terror faded quickly once I realized that I was far enough down the totem pole that whatever conclusions were drawn from these calls would be filtered down to me through my superiors. Thus began the second stage, where the unreasonable fear of having work sprung upon me was replaced by the much more rational concern that I would fall asleep in the midst of the mind-numbing chatter that surrounded me.

Eventually it happened. My nightmare was realized during one early afternoon powwow when a treacherous ray of sunlight came to a rest directly on my head. Dazzled and disoriented, I began resorting to discreetly pinching myself in an attempt to stave off the inevitable. However, the pain of the pinching stopped short of reaching my increasingly fuzzy brain. I sluggishly glanced around at my co-workers to see if they noticed the intense stifling heat of the room. All I got in return was an understanding nod from Frank, who assumed I was worn down from the conversation regarding our latest media blitz. He had no idea how close to disaster I was! A weight was rapidly descending on my head, and in a frantic effort to keep it up I balanced it on my hand as I pretended to glance down at the notes I had taken. No matter that the only thing on my pad of paper was a little stickman with a noose around his neck.

I woke up what could have been either five seconds or five minutes later. It was impossible to tell because the same never-ending subject was still being debated over the speaker phone. Complete and debilitating fear claimed my heart. I was sure I had been noticed. How could I not be noticed? I even had the tendency to snore. Had I snored and everyone was too polite to reprimand me, instead leaving it up to HR to deliver the pink slip? I had already mentally packed up my cubicle when it slowly dawned on me. Not only did no one appear to be aware, but it would make sense that no one would notice. Through all the client calls I had attended since joining the company, no one ever looked at me. I was a peon, expected to contribute nothing of value to the conversation at hand. There was no conceivable reason why anyone would feel the need to gauge my reaction, to glance over and see how Sam was handling the client's new strategy for success.

At that moment I embraced the eternal value of obscurity. I entered the third stage, largely consisting of defining the bounds of what I could achieve with my extremely low profile. I discovered I could nap for a minute at a time unscathed, and sometimes even longer. Once, after an exceptionally long slumber, I woke up to find Frank giving me a curious stare. I knew Frank wouldn't report my cardinal sin, but it did put limits on what I felt I could accomplish without being uncovered. All I had to do to compensate for my unconscious state during the meetings was to read over the post-call wrap-up email sent around to the team. It usually neatly summed up what I had been passed out for.

It was freedom, liberation from actively caring about my perception in the company. There was no perception of me in the company. Not only could I sleep, but I also could not do certain assignments if there was no fallout that could be traced back to me. I was in the office nine hours a day, but I was only mentally there half that time, doing the bare minimum to ensure my continued status as an employee. The rest of my life in the cubicle was spent engaging in the sort of tasks that made my life palatable. Whether searching online for funny videos of dogs driving cars or grading top ten album lists from music blogs, I made sure my non-work time was spent productively exploring the world beyond my desk. I was careful though. On average I would have three relevant "work" windows open for every fantasy sports webpage. You never knew when a manager-type like Donald would stroll by, curious as to what his underlings were up to, and when that did occasionally happen, I was prepared. One headphone on listening to music, the other casually dangling on my shoulder, I was always very aware of anyone in my cube's airspace, even as I engaged in an intense IM conversation with Mack concerning if there was such a such a thing as being "too high." The next time I updated my resume I was going to remember to highlight "multitasking" as a prominent skill.

It was a great shock then when I suddenly heard the words "Hey, Sam" directed at me from a few feet back. I jumped out of my seat and spun around, not even attempting to minimize the video I had playing of a Japanese man dunking on a basketball hoop via a trampoline twenty feet away. It was Lucie. In my cubicle. This was a first.

"Yo! What's up?!" I replied, noticing with some annoyance how high-pitched my voice sounded in my own ears. "Just, uh, taking a little break."

She looked over my shoulder and smiled when she saw Suzuki Takomoto's instant replay. "Impressive. Hey, we all need to relax sometimes, right? I've been so stressed this week. You know, with the Voton announcement and all."

I vaguely remembered that her client had done something special, but I had a clearer recollection of the doughnuts which had been offered at the meeting. I was always on guard for any leftovers from various functions that took place around the office. Sometimes I didn't have to buy lunch for an entire week. I would just make sure to regularly check my email for cute little messages from my coworkers saying something like "Treats in the breakroom ☺!" Then I was off. No hesitation. The best part was when others quickly descended as well, but became embarrassed when they found they were one of the first to arrive on the scene. Not me. I already had put the cream cheese on my bagel and was pouring a second glass of Starbucks coffee.

"Yeah, I usually get on top of things pretty quick," I answered with a smirk. "If I'm really diligent I find I never really get stressed out."

She gave me a long look, and I could tell she, unlike the majority of the office, saw my words for their falsity. She laughed, a really infectious giggle that stunned me with its sexiness. Maybe she thought my dumbfounded expression was on purpose, because she laughed again. For the first time I smelled her, a subtle scent that hinted of the summer to come. But better, much better.

"Anyways, Sam, I was just stopping by to let you know I'm going to be joining the Hart team. I know you're been shorthanded since Frank left to 'pursue other opportunities.'" She wore a bittersweet smile, balancing the loss of Frank, who had been her friend as well, with the hilarious monotone email notifying the employees of his departure. The email, like all the other emails letting us know of company turnover, was deliberately vague and completely bereft of feeling.

Frank Robinson has left Legacy, deciding to pursue other opportunities at this time. Frank was a valued member of the Hart, Clearlake, Freewire, and Doublepoint teams for the past two years. We appreciated his service and wish him the best in his future endeavors.

A carbon copy of every other goodbye email. Once in a while a festive executive would add something personal, as if letting us know that they knew how much Frank liked the Red Sox meant they would lose sleep that night as well. I would have preferred something juicier, something which really shed light on his character.

Frank was notorious for his hour-long bathroom breaks, even going as far as occasionally bringing a sandwich and a copy of Playboy in with him. He also occasionally returned from lunch visibly intoxicated, a bold maneuver that was a constant source of amusement to his friends.

But if Frank knew his leaving meant that Lucie would be on the Hart team with me, I have no doubt he would have high-fived me on his way out the door.

"That's great!" I replied, grinning like an idiot. "Do you want me to bring you up to speed on where we are with the client?" Why did I say that? I had no idea where we were with the client.

"Nah, Beth already sent me an email today letting me know that she would take me out to lunch and go over the basics. But thanks anyway! I think we'll have some fun together. You seem like you have a unique approach to work. I can only hope your diligence rubs off on me." Lucie gestured at the world champion trampoline dunker on my screen to emphasize to her point. She laughed again and exited my cubicle, leaving me blushing. I couldn't remember the last time I blushed, but my cheeks were burning up.

My good mood quickly soured when I checked my email again. There, at the top of my inbox, was a message from Joanne Hollis. Pete's mom. I paused, debated, then decided to double click and see what was contained within. CCed on it were Mack and Finn, and its purpose was to remind us of the upcoming memorial service on Saturday at Pete's house. We were invited, and Joanne also wanted me to say a few words commemorating his life.

I deleted the email as soon as I finished reading it. I had responded to the original invite with a polite refusal to either attend or say anything. Mack and Finn had insisted that I at least go, but that simply wasn't happening. The funeral had been bad enough. I would not be commemorating Pete's life at his house. Maybe if the service was at Fulton, in the little patch of pine trees near Youley Pond where he liked to sit and read. More than anything, I didn't want to be a part of any somber ceremony that delivered a harsh reminder of my best friend's fate. Pete's parents were serious people; Pete was not. Just unstable and self-destructive.

6

EXIT FROM THE WOMB

FOR ALL THE talk about exciting life changes, the first year out of
Fulton was surprisingly mundane. Kate and I had, in spite of our love,
decided that we should strike out on our own as single post-grads. I had
thought that since we seemed to be so great for each other maybe we
could try the whole long-distance thing, but she, with a softly patronizing
smile, had said: "Sam, don't you think we're a little too young to commit
like that? We both have so much growing to do, and I know it would be
good for me if I were able to focus on myself for a while. But we'll stay
in touch, right?"

We had tried to do just that the first few months, but distance quickly
severed our previously intimate connection. The phone calls eventually
stopped being regular, and then ceased completely. It was tough, but
whenever I started to dwell on what we had I just had to recall that she
was all too willing to throw it all away. If she didn't need me then I didn't
need her. Or any other girlfriend. This was my time to "grow as a person."
I recalled that being what college was for as well, but whatever.

In September I reluctantly left my house to move into Boston with
Mack and Finn. To say I was a little worried about being on my own
would be an understatement, but hey, everyone else was doing it. Pete was
somewhere out in California making the most of his life, so why couldn't
I do the same back East? Well, while I believed Pete was having wild times
out West, the truth was neither I nor any of our other friends had heard

from him since graduation. But we had plenty to cope with on our own and believed Pete to be the last person who needed watching over.

Both of my new roommates had been subletting in Boston that summer, so by the time I arrived they had already settled into their new lives. Finn was working his job at a lab while Mack was living off his trust fund and occasional temp jobs, both seemingly content with their post-collegiate situations. Things started off tentatively for me, as I spent my first couple of months temping downtown at the same firm that employed Mack. Any romantic notions I had had of instant success were quickly swallowed up by a healthy dose of realism, and I soon found myself without money or tangible job prospects. Growing increasingly unsure of my position, it was with great relief that I managed to secure an interview and subsequent job offer from Legacy. I was uninspired by the company, but I was also broke. I signed my contract and gladly plunged myself in the safety of corporate America.

As fall faded into winter, our post-grad life routine began to take a more concrete shape. We, excluding Mack, worked our requisite forty hours a week, often venturing out to find other Fulton grads in the city to party with. And there were plenty. Apparently year after year the number of twenty-two to thirty-year-olds in Boston from our alma mater only expanded. Thus, when new grads entered the urban haven, they already had a built-in social network they could immerse themselves in. This lack of friend diversity appeared to contradict the whole "growing as a person" philosophy everyone was espousing, but I wasn't complaining. I was uncomfortable enough with my new life and didn't want to have to get used to new friends.

Everything was more static than life at college. Your days had a more rigid structure, and those spontaneous efforts to go out during the week became rarer when winter came around. Free time was more precious than ever, but I found myself watching television during those spare moments. I had never watched TV at school, but if I had to choose between a get-together an hour away or the comfort of my couch with Mack and Finn, the couch often won out. I had never really considered how much of my personal connection with my friends at Fulton had existed because of our proximity to each other, but I quickly realized an extra half hour of travel drastically reduced face time with people I had expected to remain close with. So, despite being immersed in a sea of Fulton grads, Mack, Finn, and I only chose to regularly associate with a small fraction of them. I knew the isolation would happen eventually, but not this quick. So much had changed so fast.

Impromptu ultimate Frisbee pickup games were replaced by office birthday parties where awkward conversation was forced between bites of store-bought cake. This was a downgrade in quality of life for some. For others, it was their long-awaited heyday. All those who had hit the books long into their Saturday nights now were being accepted in law or medical schools, and the kids who refused to smoke pot found themselves aides to members of Congress.

What was occurring was a subtle shifting of priorities. Understandable, but still regrettable. Conversations at parties tended to drift to talk of salary requirements and which of our friends would get married first. The marriage talk especially was funny, until people started getting engaged. I guess I saw it coming, but as the months dragged on I didn't feel like I belonged at all to the new world I inhabited. It wasn't necessarily a bad life, but it wasn't a life I recognized as my own. I was consistently disconcerted, on edge, and disoriented. It was as though when we graduated school we all crested a mountain we had been scaling our entire lives, and now it was time to begin the treacherous descent.

The most frustrating thing about this state of affairs wasn't that I felt stuck in quicksand, but that I fully expected multiple branches to be extended in assistance. None appeared, and as a result I couldn't help but look back. I know I didn't have to feel a sense of dismay about life after Fulton, but I couldn't shake the suspicion that the best was over. I had been betrayed, but by whom or what I didn't know. There was nothing to direct my frustration at, so it settled in my stomach and began to corrode my insides. Hope wasn't lost, though. There was something that could alter everything, a force powerful enough to shake the foundations of my lethargy. The individual that had helped make life at Fulton as fantastic as it was.

I often thought of Pete, but as the darkness of winter descended on the city no one still had heard any word of him. We could only assume he was doing great things, because that was what Pete did. Every breath he took was grander than our own, and the stage his life was enacted on was nothing short of Broadway. So it was with childlike wonder that I reached into our mailbox in early February to pull out a postcard from "Beautiful Los Angeles!" It was simple and to the point.

Yo Muff, long time no see. That'll change soon enough. Keep your eyes peeled in a few months, cause I be coming in hot! Much affection, Pete

I quickly brought the letter in to Mack and Finn, who both cracked open beers in his honor. That night we crashed a party filled with Fulton alums and let the word of Pete's impending arrival spread like wildfire. Even with my crushing hangover the next morning, I couldn't help but smile. Pete was the guiding light, the one to make us forget our dull adult lives and show us the true path to happiness post-college. And he'd be here just in time for summer. The next few months were about as uneventful as the previous six, but they flew by nevertheless. It was early May when Mack, Finn, and I decided to throw a "one year out of school" party. The online invites went out weeks ahead of time, lending the impression to all of our friends and acquaintances this was no ordinary party. More than just a flimsy excuse to buy kegs, this soiree was being held to give Pete an opportunity to finally explode onto the scene and reclaim his throne.

7

THE NATIVE SON RETURNS

HE DIDN'T DISAPPOINT. I loved how he always had a knack for capitalizing on social situations to magnify the excitement at hand.

We had opened our doors early, just like we would have in college. Seven p.m. start, which meant the three of us started pre-gaming at about five. The entire day at work I had made a conscious effort to act more and more ill, until by four p.m. I had built up a respectable case to leave an hour early. I left my cubicle with thinly veiled glee, coughing repeatedly to try and mask the smile that continued emerging against my will. Frank knew what was up, as it was his example I was emulating. He saluted me as I left, briefly disengaging himself from the online dating site he had been frequenting the last couple of weeks. He had already stood up three different girls, noting that if they were on the site something must be wrong with them. He himself only joined up for the attention, which he said gave him the confidence to hit the clubs for the coming weekend. If these girls were interested in just a picture of him, imagine what the fine ladies downtown would think when they got a taste of live-action Frank.

I wished I'd had as much luck as Frank. Life in the first year away from Kate and college girls hadn't yielded much in the way of love. Like when I was a freshman in high school or a freshman in college, I was currently at the bottom of the ladder. Women in their mid-twenties wanted nothing to do with a recent grad. Of course, once I realized that I lied about my age, but words couldn't disguise the fact that I didn't know how to act like a person with five years of the "real world" under his belt. When I initiated conversations I saw by their expressions that I didn't act nearly serious enough. I made too many inappropriate jokes, acted like I couldn't care less about my employment, and generally conducted myself in a manner far too enthusiastic for their liking. I observed my older competition, the well-dressed and smooth talking gentleman who made sure to buy drinks for their prey before they whisked them away in their Audis, and concluded that it was fine to be twenty-two and immature a little longer. Plus I could barely afford five-dollar beers for myself, let alone for some happy hour honey who wanted to marry a lawyer.

I preferred house parties to the bar scene anyway. Our house, initially containing only Finn, Mack, and I, was filled with dozens of people by nine—young folks sitting around, standing up, lying down, all carrying on lively conversations without any of the outside pressure to impress one another with their status. That peace was soon disturbed when a giddy Mack dragged a keg out into the middle of the party.

"Who's doing a keg stand?!" he bellowed. "This stuff's gotta get drunk, and I want to see who's still got it!"

Silence met this request. Mack was the drunkest of anyone at the party, swaying slightly in front of the assembled partygoers, and as such everyone was prepared to ignore him until he passed out. His eyes narrowed as he realized his demand could very well go unfulfilled, and before he became belligerent and broke something I decided to take action.

"Yo Mack, I'll do one!" I called out as I walked over.

His eyes lit up. "There we go! Muffy never disappoints! Get over here bud, I'm so proud of you!" He put his arm around my shoulder and steered me to the keg. "Yo Finn, want to grab his other leg?"

Finn had been in the middle of an intense conversation with an attractive Indian girl about his plans for the future, which I guessed also included having her in his bed. He looked up as his name was called and grimaced when he saw what was happening. Ideally preferring to have nothing to do with such a juvenile endeavor, he realized we would rag him mercilessly for the next month if he fancied himself too good to help hold me up as I made a fool out of myself. He turned to the girl, gave an apologetic smile, and rose from his precious spot on the couch.

Once everyone in the crowd realized that they were no longer expected to make a scene in front of their peers, they wholeheartedly got behind the notion of my getting suspended in air. I heard cheers erupt from behind me as I was lifted and the tap was inserted between my lips. The alcohol flooded my mouth and I instinctively let my throat relax as I began to swallow.

"One! Two! Three! Four!" I heard everyone, led by Mack, yell in unison. As much as I was an unwilling participant in this debauchery, I would be damned if I didn't at least make it to twenty seconds. It was one thing to look like an idiot for doing a keg stand, it was another thing entirely to look like both an idiot and a lightweight.

"Ten! Eleven! Twelve!" The chanting had gotten louder, something I noted as I frantically tried to keep the beer going against the flow of gravity. Then, suddenly, it stopped. I felt a third pair of hands grab onto my legs and a voice call out "Thirteen! Fourteen! Fifteen!"

I spit out the tap and the hands let my legs drop to the ground. I wiped my mouth quickly and spun around. Pete stood in front of me. Just as I had remembered him. We had heard nothing of his arrival and, judging by the shocked expressions on everyone else's faces, we weren't alone in this regard.

"Hey, Muff. I'm back. Wanna get me a beer?" The last year had done much to distance me from my time at Fulton, but a brief flash of Pete's infectious grin was all it took for the memories to come rushing back.

"You son of a bitch..." was all I managed before he gathered me in a big hug. Mack and Finn came from each side and the four of us savored the moment. Once we had broken apart, everyone else came streaming in, asking the prodigal son a million questions at once about his adventures in the past year. The party had finally begun.

Eventually everyone except the four of us had drifted back to their respective dwellings. I was intrigued, for the entire night many queries had been posed to Pete about what he had been doing with himself during his absence. This was expected. The answers were not. He would smile to each eager interrogator, say briefly how glad he was to see them again, and then tell a funny story that he and that person had shared at Fulton. That individual would laugh at the fond memory and, realizing that their questions were going to be left unanswered, satisfied themselves with just being around Pete again. More than a few girls who had long pined after our returning hero asked pointed questions about his love life since heading out West, but they were rebuffed in the same manner as their male peers. If anything this only increased the mystery and appeal, and before they left they made sure he had their cell numbers.

But now it was just him and us, and I couldn't wait to absorb his last year of experience. He sat in our recliner, with Mack, Finn, and me on the couch across from him. Mack, shockingly, had stopped drinking the instant Pete had entered the party, and he was perhaps the most sober he had ever been at two on a Saturday morning. His brown eyes were wide as he waited for Pete to begin talking. Despite the five o'clock shadow he looked twelve. Finn, always the dignified patrician, nursed a glass of wine and pretended to gaze off thoughtfully into the distance, but occasionally he would betray himself and glance at Pete.

I looked right ahead at my old roommate with a mixture of amusement and worry. Something wasn't quite right. He was back, but he wasn't. Since the last partygoer had said their goodbyes a couple minutes prior, he had remained silent, preferring to look at his beer instead of us. I also had observed something vaguely disconcerting. Pete's hair was still long and full, brown locks extending over his ears and his eyes, but the few times in the course of the night when he had brushed it out of his face it had become clear his hairline had receded. Nothing too significant, but noticeable. It appeared he was going to lose his hair. I wondered how much it bothered him.

He finally spoke. "So fellas, here we are. You ready to go back to school yet?" He laughed as he said it, and we with him, but his voice had more than a little regret in it.

There was a pause, and I worried that would be all he would say. Then he began.

"The West was…informative. I'm not going to lie to you guys, but I'd appreciate it if you didn't spread this to any of our other friends." He glanced to each of us, held us with his stare for a brief second, and the words came out in a rush. Pete usually was a fast talker, but for the next few minutes the sentences poured forth like never before. We just sat, engrossed.

"I didn't exactly live the dream. I got this sweet place with a couple of other random guys just outside of L.A. and had quite a time through the summer. But my money started to run low, so I got a job at this law office in the city. I lasted a couple of weeks before I quit. My finances then being in even worse shape, I found another menial office job, this one a little better than the last. By that I mean I lasted a month before I got let go. Same story with a couple more jobs." He rubbed his nose a bit and sniffed, something he had done frequently that night, and I asked if he wanted a tissue. He gave me an undecipherable look, then shook his head. It wasn't just the receding hairline that worried me, but his general look. He seemed defeated.

"No, I'm fine, Muff. Anyway, by this time I was pretty much completely out of money, so I called home and let my parents know I was in need. Like a Christmas present. Well, maybe it was because they hadn't heard from me in months, but they weren't especially receptive to this idea. They didn't give me any additional funds, but they did get me this job with my uncle in San Bernardino. He has an orange grove there. I worked there with a bunch of Mexicans for a few months making shit for money, but at least I had free room and board with my uncle. At some point I decided I couldn't take it anymore, and that's when I sent you that postcard, Muff."

I had been frozen in place the whole time he had been telling his less-than-impressive tale, but now I nodded, desperate for him to finish this on a strong note.

"I was going to stick it out a little longer at the grove," he continued briskly. "But me and my uncle didn't quite get along and I soon found myself with just my car and a few hundred dollars. So I began my journey back East a little earlier than planned. I got the party invite yesterday when I was in Indiana, so I drove like crazy and here I am. Which reminds me, I haven't pissed in what seems like an eternity. Excuse me, gentleman." He exited his chair and made his way to the bathroom.

The three of us could have exchanged an incredulous glance. Instead, we all just stared ahead and pondered the implications of what was just relayed to us. Pete's life out of school could have been said by some to be an unmitigated disaster. No job, no money, working in an orange grove. Throughout the whole confession he appeared to be trying to verbally outrun the impact of what he was saying as if by dumping a series of unimpressive facts on us quickly enough we would be unable to put it all together. But we all knew what had been communicated. He'd just outlined a lost year.

It was not his actual experiences that incriminated him, but rather his demeanor. Throughout his talk he would have appeared shy to a stranger. We knew him better. He was ashamed. Things had not gone his way, and to what extent it was deserved, he blamed himself. The same Pete who had made college seem so refreshingly effortless now had rejoined us as a jarring failure, and looking at Mack and Finn I could see they were as disturbed as I.

Pete had three sets of eyes watching him as he strolled back into the room. He was no longer ashamed. He was bold, he was purposeful, his eyes burned with passion. He stood in front of us and cleared his throat. Rubbing his nose briefly, he made his case.

"Guys, I want to live with you next year. I want to get a job I like and I want to feel satisfied that my life is moving forward. I treaded water for the past year and it didn't really resonate with me." He smiled and winked, delivering his boyish charm with pinpoint accuracy. "So what do you think? Will you guys have me?"

That August we had found a four-bedroom and Pete was busy looking for employment. In the meantime, we paid his share of the rent between the three of us. It was the least we could do to assist our comrade in his resurrection.

8

LUCK WITH LUCIE, DANGER WITH DONALD

LUNCHTIME ARRIVED AS a blessing, because now I could drop any pretense of doing work. The act of being industrious weighed on you more than you would think. A lot of people would head outside for lunch, looking to soak in the recently strengthened rays of the sun. I had initially sought the same reprieve from the artificial office environment, spending my hour basking in the glow of something natural. But it was too much and I would get over-stimulated. I knew what would happen if I went outside. On those crisp breezes my mind would float away to the spring days in my youth. I would smell the leaves, hear laughter, and see the smiles of friends I hadn't seen in years. Then, there would be a struggle where I would barely escape from my escapism, clenching my jaw and accepting all that was around me as the bitter truth. I would stumble back inside, into the dark, and regret my excursion outside for rest of the afternoon.

I finally learned and adapted. My nervous system couldn't take any alteration of my comatose workday, so I caged myself. No leaving the office, no trips to the outside world unless I was being accompanied by a coworker. I contented myself with exploring the wider world through the medium of the Internet, with the promise of fresh air looming as an incentive to get me through the rest of my day.

Try as I might to carve out a lunchtime island, there were obstacles. People would send emails asking folks if they wanted to bring their lunches out to the kitchen and socialize, and I was unfortunately included on these emails. This was not something I would have been inclined to be a part of, but if I didn't want to be noticed it was best not to be seen as the office loner. I had friends in the office, buddies with whom I would socialize, but there was no quality control in these lunch emails. My friends Dan, Meg, and Henry would be on the same list as Greg, Michaela, and Kelly, three people who I couldn't stand. Sadly, today was a day when I had received a lunch invite.

I had immediately deleted it and hoped I wouldn't be asked why I had not made it, but that fervent wish was dashed upon the rocks at quarter of one when I heard: "Hey man, how's it going?!"

I slowly took off my headphones and turned to face Greg Shannon, standing there attempting to look rather aloof, as if the enthusiasm of his words had ruined his image. Well-dressed in a cheap sort of way, Greg was a young man who had completely bought into whatever it was corporate America was selling. His physique was perhaps the most impressive thing about him, a result of him hitting the gym regularly before work every day. But all the exercise in the world wouldn't make him pretty. In keeping with his professional image he kept his hair short and face clean-shaven, but that just brought more attention his weak chin and too-long nose.

This was a man who took his job seriously, but that didn't stop him from trying to relax with his "peers." Watching him try to navigate social waters was humorous for about five minutes. Then it just wore you down.

"Yo, Greg, what's up?" I don't know why, but I still held out some hope he wouldn't bring up the lunch email. Maybe I wasn't completed jaded yet.

"Hey Sam, just checking to see if you got that email I sent you regarding lunch. The rest of us are already out there."

I turned back to my computer screen and made a show of looking at my email. After conducting a studious search to locate the email I had deleted, I turned back to him with an apologetic smile.

"Oh, this morning's been absolutely nuts with the Hart team, I must have missed it. You guys are eating right now, huh? Well, let me grab my tuna sandwich and I'll be there in a minute." I gave an enthused look and it seemed to satisfy him as he marched off in the direction of the kitchen. With agonizing slowness I lifted myself from my chair and made my way after him, the sound of telephones and typing surrounding me in a hypnotic cacophony. I fought the urge to run.

The kitchen was livelier, with multiple groups of my coworkers chatting away about celebrities, sports, or romance. It seemed as though everyone was getting engaged or impregnated as of late, so that provided much in the way of conversation starters.

I spotted my group in the corner. Lucie was sitting on the end of the booth, and when she saw me she smiled, moving in to allow me to sit next to her. Since when was she on these lunch emails? I felt a little seasick.

"Hiiii Sam. How aarrrrrrre you?" This was Michaela—tall, blond, and gorgeous, with a smile that couldn't help but make you giddy. This was a smile that lacked any uncertainty; she beamed it out with an intuitive awareness of her own beauty. She had nothing to fear and she knew it.

I gave her a thumbs-up in response and she laughed. But she wasn't done examining me.

"Are you growing a *beard*?!" This was in response to the week's worth of stubble I had been accumulating, and she was acting like this was some dirty secret between just the two of us.

"Yeah, I'm thinking about it." This is what I always said, and I always ended up shaving after a week or so. A guy with a beard would attract attention.

"Cool!" Her feigned excitement made me wince, but I managed to look flattered.

There was another thing about Michaela. She was completely uninteresting in the worst sort of way because she, at least superficially, thought she was interesting. I wondered, deep down, if she harbored doubts about her own value as a person. Did she lay awake at night and try to consider what she delivered to any interpersonal relationship she was a part of? And did she end each internal debate by promising herself that she would buy a new perfume the next day? In a weird way her complete dullness fascinated me, especially the way she dealt with it through language. Everything was exaggerated, especially things that definitely were anything but interesting. It's like she felt a duty to make her life appear more noteworthy than it actually was. I settled down to listen to her conversation with Kelly, which restarted after we had settled the beard question.

"So Sam, me and Kelly were just talking about the *craziest* thing last night, weren't we Kelly?"

Kelly was also pretty, sporting the same long blond hair and blue eyes. She lacked the megawatt movie star smile, but she also seemed to possess some of the substance Michaela was missing. She didn't start her answers to questions with a blank look and put forth her own opinions on subjects not related to *US Weekly*. Sadly, the allure Michaela held for men seemed to have convinced Kelly that being Michaela was a better alternative than being Kelly. Maybe she was right. I don't know if I had a better solution for her.

"Totally! It was *insane*. You guys won't believe it." Our silence and Greg's enthusiastic nodding apparently was all they needed for approval.

"So me and Kelly went to this club last night to go dancing..." Michaela spoke quickly, almost seeming to strain for breath, smiling after every pause. I think she thought that each break lent a sort of drama to the story, but it just made it more frustrating for everyone subjected to it. I fervently hoped this tale would be better than the last one, which had climaxed with her telling how the shoe store clerk had told her Cameron Diaz had just bought the same pair of shoes yesterday. I had laughed out loud, unable to keep to myself my opinion of the absurdity I faced. Thankfully, Michaela and Kelly (who had been blown away by the tale) thought it was the laughter of one who had garnered joyous pleasure from the event, so they smiled knowingly at my reaction.

"And we're waiting at the bar for some guys to buy us drinks when we see Beth Joseph come in with Sam!" Michaela continued, oblivious to the look of horror emerging on my face. I had underestimated the impact a dumb blond could have on my life. Michaela was staring right at me, smiling her bright white smile, ecstatic that she was the one breaking this great news to the group.

"Umm, I don't remember going to any club last night," I countered, not daring to look in the direction of Lucie. "You sure it wasn't someone else?" I refused to try to make it seem like I was embarrassed or worried by what Michaela thought she saw, but I stared at her intensely enough that some of that smile left her face. Confused by my lack of excitement at having this news told to our friends, she sojourned on.

"No, it was definitely you!" she responded after a brief pause, refusing to let go of her tabloid tale. "Kelly saw it too!"

"I did! You two looked like you were having a *great* time." Kelly made sure to emphasize the word great, as if everyone hadn't already noticed where they were going with this. Now that Kelly had contributed her two cents, Michaela once again seized the reins.

"So we yelled out at you two and told you to come over, but you both seemed really buuuusy." Michaela winked again. Was that even necessary at this point? This was a pretty bad development. Everyone was looking at me, with varying expressions. Greg had some kind of newfound respect for the guy who got with management, but rather than make me hate him it made me feel more disgusted with myself. Meg, Dan, and Henry were all regarding me with detached amusement, not as much surprised as they were curious to see how I would respond.

I finally let my eyes focus on Lucie. She also looked curious, but not amused, which I was grateful for. At least that meant she cared. It also meant that if I wanted to save whatever I might have with her I had to do damage control. I made a conscious effort not to address her specifically, but the only reason I was going to say anything was because of her.

"Um, yeah, I ran into her last night and we never really had got to know each other out of work, so we talked for a while." I hoped that would suffice, but by the looks of everyone seated I had to give them more.

"Nothing really happened. I don't like her or anything, and I'd be surprised if we even hang out again. Sorry to disappoint." Everyone was still giving me suspicious looks, but they were willing to let it drop. Thank god. I headed back to my desk soon after, citing all the work I had piled up. Unable to stop myself, I attempted to make eye contact with Lucie again as I waved goodbye, but she was being grilled by Kelly about her tastes in clothes.

One good thing emerged out of lunch. For the first time in a long while, I had in my possession an ounce of resolve. I was going to ask Lucie out.

As the workday finally ground its way to a halt, I gathered up my belongings and quickly headed over to her end of the office, fingers crossed the whole time. I needed this to work.

I walked and tendrils of fear worked their way down my throat to my heart. I welcomed them. The sweaty palms and quick breaths meant I was alive. When you're a teenager, every new girl makes lightning run up and down your spine. You don't really know what you're doing, you don't know how she'll react, and your imagination will whisk you away before you can stop it. Then, when the climactic moment finally arrives, you always feel grateful and a little surprised because, no matter how confident you may have appeared, you weren't sure things would fall into place.

Most people lose this naiveté at some point in their life. They learn to read the signs, they learn to play the game. They know what means yes and what means no and how certain things about their looks or their status will undeniably appeal to the opposite sex. It pained me not only to admit I knew what angle to take to get a girl into bed, but that I usually felt a sense of power and satisfaction when I succeeded. There is something to be said for the lost days of pubescence where failure was commonplace but success always felt like Christmas morning.

Rounding the corner to her cubicle, I immediately realized I should have thought it through a little more. She was just about to leave, getting up from her chair right as I halted in front of her. Everything went blank and I just stared. For about five seconds. She stared back, eyes wide. Things had just gotten really intense. I jumped in the deep end.

"Hey, you wanna chill tomorrow night? Like a movie or dinner or something along those lines?" This was a nightmare. I wanted to push her out of the way and hide under her desk until the lights went out. My eyes remained locked on hers, if only because every muscle in my entire body was jammed in place. I watched as those eyes smiled, and followed that smile down to her mouth.

"I can't see that being a problem," she said, moving closer to me and taking my hand in hers. Still smiling, she wrote her number on my palm. You could have convinced me in that moment that I loved her, but all I could fathom was her soft small hands lightly grasping mine as I felt the pen tip weave its way across my skin.

"There!" she said, letting my hand fall limply to my side as she looked back up at me. "So I'll see you tomorrow night?"

"Can't wait. Take it easy."

"Bye, Sam."

I stood there for a second, savoring it, then started moving towards the elevator. I had already peaked; time to escape before things derailed. I spun around and called out: "What kind of food do you like?" She had been watching me leave and I thought there was nothing sweeter than seeing that. She looked upwards and bit her lip, then answered.

"Thai!"

"Thai it is!" We both waved again and I jogged to the rapidly closing elevator. I barely caught it, and for an instant I was in such a euphoric stupor I thought I was alone inside. That loving haze quickly dissipated when I my fellow occupant. Vice-president Donald. Staring at me. Or rather through me. Happiness is such a fragile thing.

I was surprised at how good-looking he was. His gray hairs only added to his mystique, and though he was thirty years my senior it was apparent he was in much better shape. I could also see how his penetrating eyes, a dark brown, had the potential to be welcoming. I highly doubted I would see the realization of the potential.

We had twenty floors together, and he didn't waste any time.

"Hey there, I've seen you around the office but I don't think I know your name. I'm Donald." His hand was already extended. I took it and got the expected extra-firm shake. He contorted his stern mouth into a surprisingly disarming smile, and I instinctively found myself wanting to impress him.

"My name's Sam."

"Sam." Donald tasted the word like a fine wine, feeling it for texture and flavor. His face gave away his conclusion. Not nearly aged enough, and clearly had been a substandard batch of grapes to begin with.

"Yeah, I work under Beth Garcia. I've been here for a couple of years." That seemed to disturb him mildly, like I was a cockroach who had been living in his kitchen unnoticed.

"Do you like it here, Sam? Is Legacy working out well for you?" He was acting mildly interested, as if he was simply making conversation, but I knew I was on the stand.

"Well, I think this job is the perfect fit for my skill set. I've found both the work and the people here to be just great and I really feel like I've learned so much." That comment made him blanch a little; I doubt he thought I would have understood what I was required to do in this situation. But it wasn't dumb luck that had kept me employed here. I continued to receive my salary because I knew what had to be said and what appearance had to be maintained.

"So you see yourself here in the foreseeable future?" He managed to force almost all of the incredulity out of his voice.

"I feel like working here has been such a positive experience that I can't imagine leaving anytime soon. I really feel grateful to have been a part of the company's success the last two years." The lies slipped so easily through my teeth.

A brief quiet ensured, where Donald double-checked with himself that I was indeed bullshitting him. I had to be. I didn't look the part, and the way I carried myself belied my words. He had already made his decision, and men like Donald were not used to rethinking their assumptions. That is what made them successes. They had confidence in their abilities and, deserved or not, it colored them positively in front of their peers, who wanted to believe that men like Donald had the character they lacked. It was just a group of men in suits masturbating each other's egos. And while they might never admit it, they liked it better than sex. Because they could be sure of the approbation of the other parties involved.

"Well, Sam," Donald said as he put a hand good-naturedly on my shoulder, "I look forward to observing your progress at Legacy. The best way for you to get move up the ladder here would be if your work received personal attention from management. I'll ask to be CCed on your subsequent efforts for this company." He looked at me like he expected me to be honored, even though he knew that I knew he thought I was a punk. This Donald, he hoped to be liked even as he attempted to weed me out. People are complicated, I suppose, and there is no reason why Donald would be any different.

I felt really tired just then. I thanked Donald for his taking an interest in my work and how I hoped he would find it to his liking. As we exited the elevator, he walked to the front door and I excused myself to the men's room. When I got inside I slowly made my way over to the sinks, putting a hand on either side of one to brace myself. Slowly raising my head I ventured a look at my reflection, trying to stifle the vague sense of dread building up inside of me. All I saw was a pair of blank, desperate eyes. Nothing else mattered, just those frantic, confused pools in my face. I became enveloped in them; I went for a swim in their terror-filled waters. Finding that I couldn't drown, I jerked my head away and left the bathroom, not taking a breath until I left the office. Then I vomited a little in the back of my throat. I always hated when that happened.

As I drove home I was confronted by the setting sun, spraying its fading light directly into my field of vision. I didn't look away. I forced my eyelids open and stared straight ahead until all I could see was white. Keeping my foot on the accelerator, I waited for the blindness to subside, which it eventually did. The burning orb slowly took shape and I found I quickly was able to define its boundaries.

I remembered when our teachers brought us outside to watch a solar eclipse in third grade. They gave us sunglasses and warned us to beware of looking too long at the star in the sky. I had been afraid of going blind and had only stared up briefly, in awe of a force so powerful. Not any longer. Now I boldly gazed as the sun's last remaining rays crossed the horizon. But there was no satisfaction. I didn't care anymore. The myth had evaporated, and now all that mattered was the darkness I saw creeping across the sky.

9

VOYAGE TO FULTON

"I NEVER SHOULD have gone back." Pete said over his shoulder as he pulled the pot off the stove. Canned chicken noodle soup again. He said he was getting heartburn, and I believed him. I didn't eat well, but I had watched him consume many meals and there was no way his diet wasn't eroding the lining of his stomach. To my knowledge, he hadn't had a fresh vegetable in months.

I stared at him, waiting a few seconds before responding: "Yeah." I didn't know what else to say. It had been a rough ride back rough for all of us. Especially Pete.

We hadn't said much the trip back from Fulton. He, Mack, and I had all gone up to our alma mater for homecoming weekend, thinking it would be good to get back to our roots. Finn had refused. Said there was no way he was heading back to school for a weekend.

"Guys, we graduated a year and a half ago. Let it go. School was great but I've moved on. Enjoy yourselves. I'm sure it's the same as it always was. Plus, I need to study for the MCATs."

"Didn't you already take them?" Pete had asked.

"Nope. Not yet. Making sure I really know the course material inside and out before I do. I want to ace them and be a lock at my reach schools."

"Then why call them 'reach schools'?" Mack had muttered under his breath as we exited the apartment.

Ignoring Finn's words, we set off in the highest spirits. None of us had been back since graduation and we knew a bunch of this year's seniors. Good times awaited us.

Pete had a job now, working in a marketing firm downtown. I had met some of his coworkers and they all seemed to be enamored of him. I hadn't found that surprising, but I was curious as to how Pete presented himself in a corporate setting. How was the consummate college kid reacting to a world of cubicles and business casual? Their answers revealed a great deal, especially since none of them were his superiors.

They had told me he was great because he was the guy who vocalized all their dissatisfactions at work. He'd send biting emails about absurd work policies and always tried to get everyone off-topic at meetings. They could always count on him to break up the monotony of the day, and for that alone they loved him. Apparently, despite blatantly undermining their authority, his superiors couldn't stay mad at him either. As long as he did his work they were willing to put up with Pete Hollis's antics, if only because he raised team morale. I suspected an underlying motive for their tolerance being more juvenile; they also wanted to be seen as "cool" by Pete.

Sadly, this Pete, the mischievous wise-ass they were describing, never made it home. The Pete in our apartment after work every day was a ghost. I came home at the finale of my nine-to-five expecting to have Pete's presence infusing my living space. Instead, I got a quiet "Hey, dude" and the sound of soup boiling on the stove. Mack's new temp job had him working late, and Finn often stayed at the lab until eight, so it was just me and my best friend for a couple of hours every night during the week.

At work I was usually removed from the world around me, my eyes' only brightness coming from the reflection of my computer screen. However, as it did every day, five o'clock would arrive and I would make my escape. Most days when that happened I instantly became reanimated, the clean outside air (especially in the summer months) awakening my brain from its hibernation. Only then I remembered I was Sam Orcutt, who liked his fellow human beings and having fun. This change was sudden and powerful, and by the time I made it home I was usually a reasonable approximation of the kid I had been for four years at Fulton.

But Pete, just a month into his corporate existence, looked eviscerated in the evenings. I was reasonably sure it wasn't the actual stress of his job either. He seemed beaten, a man who was only breathing because his body demanded it. He wouldn't talk about work. He wouldn't talk about anything. At least for the first hour. After an hour of sitting side by side on the couch watching TV, something in him invariably responded to my presence. He would finally make some sarcastic comment about Lucie and if I had finally managed to blink in her general direction, and I would know I had him back for another day. By the time Mack and Finn came home he would be in fine spirits and we would chill out together in the common room, all of us but Pete recapping our days and whether or not we wanted to head out that night.

They were never aware of the other Pete, the glass-eyed one I met every time I came home. I believed if it had been them who came home first he wouldn't have allowed himself to be seen like that. With me there didn't have to be an explanation or any false pretensions of happiness. He knew I understood he wasn't content, and also that I wouldn't question why. I couldn't question because I was scared and selfish. I was not going to openly acknowledge that Pete was not right, because if I did that I honestly doubted I could handle what was plaguing him. I barely had a grasp on my life.

The conventional wisdom amongst our friends, all of us a year out of school, was that many people had it rough those initial years out of college, but by the time a few birthdays had passed you were well on your way to becoming a success. Thing is, Pete had already been a success in his eyes. Now, his first fall with us in Boston, I had the unwanted privilege of watching a friend torment himself with visions of his presumed golden years. Whenever he would talk of Fulton it was with a bittersweet, melancholic tone, his voice desperately trying to recreate the past. All of us missed college, even Finn, so we joined him in his wistful remembrance, but with Pete it was different. His old life was devouring him.

The voyage up to Fulton was one long trip down memory lane. We spent the whole ride retelling college stories we already knew by heart, but the fact we were headed back to the place of their origin gave them new life. The large majority of the tales were happy ones, but even the sadder recollections brought rueful grins to our faces. In hindsight they all seemed like events that had helped us grow as people.

Pete, in particular, was in rare form. He had taken that day off from work and spent it resting up, as well as getting in touch with current Fulton students he knew and finding out what was happening the two nights we were going to be up. He informed Mack and I he had already found off-campus houses for the three of us to crash in and that there would be plenty of parties to attend. Never ceasing to surprise, during the drive Pete told a few stories even I somehow hadn't heard before. I think he had been saving them for journeys back to Fulton, because they all involved current seniors and made Mack and I pumped to see these people.

We rounded the bend towards campus around eight and slowly let it soak in. Driving past familiar dorms, familiar streets, and even some familiar faces, we savored it all. Pete pulled into student parking and we saw an array of Fulton stickers on the vehicles around us. He stopped the car, put it in park, and spun towards the two of us. In the shadowy car I could see his eyes and his teeth both reflecting the light of the distant street lamps. Then he spoke, the delight barely disguised.

"Gentlemen. I've been looking forward to this for a while. I doubt it will disappoint. Let's go." And with that, we exited the car and made our way over to the campus. Fulton was situated in a small town where the college was the nexus of any social activity and, quite unlike Boston, this town was quiet already. No screaming neighbors or honking cabs, just stillness. But up ahead we already heard the occasional yell or laugh, and as we got closer we made out figures walking or running across the quad, their shadows appearing long in the lights from the surrounding halls and dorms. Each sound was more pronounced here, amplified as a result of the surrounding silence. I could make out each voice, and I even recognized some. But it wasn't just the sounds ahead that were clear. My worries had fled and my thoughts had crystallized. I looked to my left and right and saw the same relaxed, fulfilled look on Mack and Pete's faces. We weren't aimless wanderers any longer. During that fleeting moment we grasped something profound. If you asked us afterwards we couldn't have defined it, but just knowing we could still possess it was a welcome revelation. Pete called out to some girl he recognized and the weekend began.

The day and two nights we spent back at school felt like a week. During that time, mildly troubling truths emerged. That initial feeling of peace when we first entered wasn't proven incoherent when we left; it was the emotional residue of our own time at Fulton. But we quickly came to understand our perception of the campus wasn't accurate in real time. College still encapsulated all that was wonderful with the world, but it wasn't our playground any longer. It belonged to them, the underclassmen that infiltrated every party we went to. The seniors we knew were still having a great time, but they were already looking ahead and more interested in talking to us about what awaited them in the next life. Well, superficially interested. I could sense that they, much like we had been, were still deep within the collegiate bubble. But they knew, like we had, that it would end soon. So they brought us beers and asked to hear tales from beyond the grave.

The freshmen and sophomores could care less. The boys stumbled around sporting big sloppy grins, while the girls singled out older guys lounging around. They were completely enveloped by what was unfolding around them, their vision not extending past this night. Seeing them overwhelm the parties looking for beer and sex was hilarious, as was seeing the upperclassmen flaunting their limited maturity when faced with a complete lack of it.

Even as we enjoyed the spectacle, it was obvious that there was a substantial gulf between us and them. These were not our peers any longer. We could see ourselves in these collegians, but mostly they were personas we had left behind. I felt equal parts anthropologist and partygoer, observing that around me with a critical eye I hadn't before possessed. I didn't feel wise, but I did feel removed. It was great seeing Fulton still functioning as a realm in which another generation of kids were finding themselves, and I appreciated how it had done the same for me, but now it could only serve as a reprieve from my current situation. Our nostalgia was tempered by cold reality, and we found our fuzzy feelings of the past placed into perspective. What we had was beautiful while we had it, but these were not our friends and this was not our Fulton. We had moved on, but I don't know if any of us could tell the others where to.

These conclusions, dimly felt in the intoxication, wouldn't really cut until the ride back. However, there was one discovery that immediately made an impact on me. In the early morning hours of that Saturday I lost track of Pete. Mack had been making the most of his time back and found himself in the arms of a freshman girl. I wasn't sure why it wasn't the other way around, but seeing a 250-pound man perched on the lap of a girl half his size was visually rewarding in a way I wouldn't have thought possible. He was too drunk to realize he was crushing her and she was doing an admirable job of pretending that he wasn't. After fifteen minutes of mocking that situation with other passersby, I looked around the house we were at and didn't see Pete anywhere. I asked and was told he was in the basement. An hour ago I would have had to fight my way through hordes of kids to reach the basement but, as it was almost two, the crowd had thinned out enough to allow me quick passage.

Despite diminished numbers, the remaining partygoers seemed to be creating a significant amount of noise, and when I began my descent down the stairs I realized the majority of the sound had been originating below. There were about a dozen kids, including Pete, sitting in a circle around a mirror. On the mirror rested a small mountain of cocaine. Well aware that a fair number of kids at Fulton dabbled in coke, I had always steered clear. Surrounded by so many types of alcohol as well as a bounty of weed, I didn't see the need to experiment in another form of mental destruction. Pete had also, to my knowledge, never used coke, so it was with a vague sense of unease that I watched him roll up a twenty-dollar bill and snort one long line of the white powder. He rubbed his nose quickly and glanced up to see me standing across the room.

It could have been a serious moment, but I wouldn't allow it. I was tired of seriousness, of sorrow. It was just some coke. He could handle himself. I mocked his nose rubbing in my own frantic way and he laughed from across the room. It was a happy laugh, and for that I was grateful. I walked over and he introduced me to a sophomore named Eva, whose dilated eyes rarely left his face. I looked at her closely and realized something. She looked remarkably like Nora. Same long, wavy blond hair, same eyes, same nose.

"Eva is Nora's younger sister," Pete said as he saw my bemused expression. "We hung out a few times when I stayed at Nora's."

"Nora still talks about you," Eva said, with the same appealing enthusiasm Nora projected. "She wanted to know why Pete hasn't been staying in touch." She looked at Pete accusingly, and for an instant he looked profoundly uncomfortable. He twitched a little bit, shrugged, and cracked a smile which quickly dissipated.

"I'll get around to it. Just been so busy. I'm sure she's got another guy anyways."

He didn't look at Eva when he talked, and it hit me. He still loved her. It was hard to read him due to the effects of the coke, but I had known him a long time and could recognize when he was unnerved. His eyebrows tended to rise up a little and, just like now, his gaze went anywhere but the object that disturbed him.

Eva laughed. "She's had a couple of guys over there at Oxford, but she drops them pretty quick. Says they're too full of themselves over there." Her face took on a more somber look. "I think she misses you."

Things had quickly become real awkward. Pete's expression became even more agitated, the combination of cocaine and news about Nora clearly overwhelming him. It didn't help that the messenger looked so eerily similar to his old girlfriend. I helped diffuse the situation by asking Eva about her classes. She was majoring in "cultural production," and, in the time it took for her to explain exactly what that was, Pete had collected his bearings and managed to ask her a few follow-up questions. I knew he would eventually pull himself together; he was too much of a social butterfly to ever cause a scene. Reassured, I made my exit.

"Okay, dude, I was just checking in to make sure you hadn't gotten lost and you're not lost, so I'll be heading to find a nice couch to crash." I said this as I grabbed him by the shoulders and nodded towards Eva. "Nice to meet you, Eva." She smiled brightly back and put her arm around Pete.

"Don't worry, I'll take good care of him." Pete looked at ill ease with this gesture but managed a good-natured grin when Eva glanced over at him.

"Yeah dude, Eva will lay out my game plan for winning Nora back. With her on my side I'm guaranteed success." They both high-fived and we all laughed, me hoping mine didn't sound as forced as it felt. Waving goodbye, I proceeded to stumble back up the stairs. I had been so focused on Pete that I had forgotten how drunk I was. Clumsily navigating my way though the house, I eventually found a futon in a back room where I could sleep. I curled up and willed the room to stop spinning.

Eventually it did, but then a single thought escaped through my drunken haze. The Pete downstairs with Eva wasn't Fulton Pete anymore. I had had the utmost faith that Fulton Pete was destined for something special, but starting with graduation night, that faith had been steadily declining. He had been a lighthouse for me, but now his guiding beam was growing dim. I couldn't decide who I was more afraid for: me or him. And I didn't know how to begin bringing this up to him. Right now we could pretend we were fine, and there was some solace in that. But the instant we tried to address what was wrong the illusion crumbled, and with it the underlying sense of invincibility we had possessed upon leaving school. It was latent, something we wouldn't discuss unless we wanted to feel like entitled pricks. We had grown up expecting greatness to be thrust upon us. We were the vanguard of our generation, the cream of the crop, and our acceptance into Fulton had only solidified that impression. To admit that my expectations had far exceeded my pathetic accomplishments was something I couldn't stomach. The fire inside of us, the ambition to succeed, was sputtering, and I wasn't sure how it could be reignited if it disappeared completely.

I stared into space for what seemed like hours. It was probably two minutes. Then the door to the room creaked open and a face peeked in. It was a girl.

"Oh, are you sleeping back here?" she asked, slurring the 'here' slightly.

"Yeah, I'm just visiting some friends and I needed a place to crash." I focused my attention on the ceiling, lest the room begin to rotate again. I heard the door open a little more and a thin beam of light illuminated the small female form that tentatively advanced towards my futon.

"You're Pete Hollis's friend, aren't you?" She was close now, and in the dim light I thought I recognized her. I couldn't remember her name, but I think she had been a freshman when we graduated, which would make her a junior now.

"Yeah, I'm Sam. Pleased to meet you." I extended my hand and she took it, shaking it lightly and slowly releasing it from her own.

"I'm Amy. You might not remember me, but I was a freshman when you graduated. My older brother Ian was in your class." I recalled Ian. He was a colossal douchebag, a lacrosse player who landed an investment banking job out of school with some significant help from his father. His sister I remembered as being really cute, if a little promiscuous.

"Yeah, I remember Ian. Good guy. I hear he's doing well."

"Yep! He's down in New York." There was a pause. Then I heard her voice soften a little. "This is actually my friend Lily's house. I stay here a lot when I party because I live across campus. Would you mind if I shared the futon with you tonight?"

And just like that, thoughts of anything but sex were banished from my head.

"Uhh, yeah. I'm sure I can make room." I scooted over and she crawled in. Her hair had a slight floral scent. Her breath smelled of Pabst.

*****

We drove home Sunday morning, not looking back as we left the campus behind. Mack spent the entire ride sleeping off his substantial hangover, but only after giving a play-by-play of his second night with the freshman girl, whose name he couldn't remember anymore. He would get emails from her for the next two months. They were hilarious, with her insinuating they should seriously consider a long-term commitment.

Pete and I rode in silence, listening to his iPod play through the radio. Saturday night I had lost him again, but this time I hadn't gone looking. After a while he had resurfaced and we went for a late-night walk around campus, talking of the past. He occasionally rubbed his nose as we mused about old friends and old memories, and I did my best to ignore it. Now he looked like shit, but we both knew that it could be worse. He could not have me next to him, transparently feeling the same malaise. Eventually I couldn't take the quiet anymore and forced myself to sleep.

Now, back at the apartment, I watched him eat his soup. Sunday night. Monday and the work week were just hours away. I was already winding down mentally, steeling myself for five more days of half-assed production. He spooned the processed meat and noodles into his mouth, chewing and staring at the football game on the screen in front of him. It was time for bed. I raised myself off the couch we both were sitting on and stretched. Without thinking I turned to him and clasped his shoulder. Tried to think of something to say and failed. He looked up and met my uncertain gaze. After a second he let loose that trademark smile. It was sincere, because he was doing it for my benefit. He turned his face back to the screen and I let go. I walked away from him and entered my bedroom, setting my alarm and quickly crawling into bed. As I drifted off to sleep I could hear a distant ambulance siren juxtaposed with the sound of Pete washing his dishes. Eventually both stopped and all I could hear was my music. Just like every other night, I let it whisk me away to nothing.

10
JUST ANOTHER THIRSTY THURSDAY

THINKING ABOUT BOTH Lucie and Donald, I pulled into my driveway. After letting the song on my iPod finish I grabbed my stuff and made my way to the front door. Even though it was seven o'clock, our first-floor apartment still looked dark inside. I heard a girl laugh and turned to look down my street. Three-floor building after three-floor building, each with multiple apartments. Some with families, but most with young professionals like myself. Even more so than at school, I occupied a space teeming with humanity. I saw couples going for walks, kids playing with each other, and tons of twenty-somethings squeezing the most out of their spare time. I wasn't alone. I was far from it.

Yet, I couldn't shake the nagging feeling of isolation that had dogged my steps for almost three years. The world around me wasn't hostile, but I couldn't detect my niche in it. I had finally been unable to avoid the inevitable conclusion that the city was my home, but realizing that hadn't diminished my unease. Turning back towards my door I felt a profound desire for Mack or Finn to be inside, but even more than that I needed for Pete to still be alive. Sighing, I turned the knob and entered the silent house.

After finishing a banana and peanut butter sandwich I cracked open a beer and a book. It had been a great read so far, but with only fifty pages left I found myself unwilling to continue. Before long, in perhaps under an hour, I would have finished it and once again be left empty-handed. Thankfully, my phone started vibrating and I was able to postpone the finale. It was my parents. I wasn't in the mood to talk to them, but I rarely was. They were a constant reminder of my own dissatisfaction with where I was. And if I didn't answer now they would just get worried and continue leaving voicemails until I finally called back.

"Hello," I answered, carefully maintaining my tone so as to allow no impatience to enter it. It would be almost impossible to continue this throughout the entire conversation, but it was always worth a shot.

"Hey Sam, it's Mom. How are you doing?" What to say to this? That was always the greatest peril of talking to Mom and Dad. They loved me and they wanted to know I was doing well. There would be nothing wrong with this were I doing well, but I hadn't been "well" for a while, and it made each interrogation a chore.

"Doing alright." There was a pause before my mom realized I had nothing to add to that. That wouldn't stop her though. She was relentless, digging tenaciously for any new facts.

"Well, how has work been this week?" She always sounded like she thought it would be different each week than it had been for the last dozen weeks, and the dozen weeks before that. I always responded:

"Same old same old. You know how it is." And she almost always answered back with:

"Well, if you don't like it you should use your free time to look for another job. Did you get those job clippings from the newspaper that I sent you?"

"Yeah, Mom, I got them. Legal aide and copywriter, right?"

"You should get on them. I don't think there is much time to apply."

"I just don't think I would really like either of those jobs." Another pause.

"Well, you could always go back to school. That might be exactly what you need. You could go and get a law degree! You would make a great lawyer." She had said this countless times as well.

"I'll consider it, but I just don't think it's what I want right now."

"Hey son, how's it going?" My dad had picked up the other line. "You see the game last night?" I could always count on him to put me back in comfortable territory. Sports were a welcome diversion, safely removed from my own life.

"Going fine, Dad, and yeah I saw it. I can't believe Troy sunk that three. He's turning out to be a hell of a player."

"I fell asleep at the half, but I saw some highlights. I'm liking what I'm seeing this year." My mother would always stay silent during these exchanges, but after we had finished she jumped back in the conversation, giving me new news concerning grandparents, aunts, uncles, and cousins I hadn't seen since college.

Throughout all this my thoughts drifted to the many moments in my adolescence where my parents looked at me with pride. Top student in high school, accepted into an elite college which fit me like a second skin, I knew they weren't losing any sleep over my progress in life then. But now whenever we talked there was a hint of worry in their voices, an uncertainty that hung in the air when I went home. They weren't sure where things had gone wrong, and despite their best efforts they couldn't set my life right. I was outside their realm of influence. Their child had gone out into the world, and the only way they could have any discernible impact on my life would be if I returned home. And I was not doing that. As I had found out with Fulton, there was no going back.

More than anything, I wanted the secure and purposeful lives they appeared to be leading. My mom was a nurse, my dad a teacher, and as far as I knew both of them always planned on having careers in those respective fields. They weren't always happy with their jobs, as evidenced by the daily complaints over the dinner table about the frustrating bureaucracies inherent in each profession, but if you had asked them (and I had) if they were happy with their chosen career paths, they always answered in the affirmative. They had entered their jobs after college, and both had no regrets about the thirty-plus years they had been engaging in their work. I used to take it for granted that I too would have this sense of satisfaction, but what if my mom and dad were two of the lucky ones? What if I was lacking in the determination and drive that allowed them to realize their passions? Maybe I resembled them in appearance alone, that somehow during conception I had failed to inherit the better parts of their DNA.

It's a great thing when you can honestly say that your parents are your role models. It could mean that they are exemplary people, leading citizens who leave an indelible imprint on the world. If Chelsea Clinton says she looks up to her parents, it is obvious why. However, if your average son or daughter, someone like myself, says that their parents are their role models, it means that that child understands the sacrifices their parents made to ensure their offspring were raised in a nurturing and loving environment. They realize how difficult it is to be responsible for the welfare of another human being, how easy it is to take that duty for granted, and how lucky they were to have their particular parents watching over them. Linked to this gratitude is the understanding that you owe your children the same, but I had nagging suspicions that the childhood I had been graced with might be beyond that grasp of my own hypothetical offspring. If I was fortunate I would find out I was sterile and not fail my own kids like I was currently failing myself.

My mom was telling me about my cousin's new baby when another call came in. It was Mack. I let my parents know I had a call I had to take and we said our goodbyes, with me promising to call them next week.

"Yo dude, where you at?" I asked.

"Out at O'Connors's! Pretty hammered right now!" He yelled over the background noise. "Tom, Ben, and their roomies are here. Some cute girls too! Get off your ass and come out!" Both Tom and Ben had been pretty close with Pete at Fulton, and I hadn't seen them in a few months. Plus, my killer hangover from the night before had faded a few hours ago.

"Yeah dude, I'll catch a cab out there. See you in a half hour."

I put on a song to pump me up and grabbed the half-finished handle of vodka from last night. Quickly downed three shots before the song finished and walked outside to hail a cab. By the time one stopped to pick me up I was already feeling the alcohol coursing through my veins, giving me that familiar numb sense of hope. I ambled into O'Connors a half hour later as promised to find Mack already stumbling around. He led me over to the bar where we each took a few more shots. Tom and Ben found us and we all took some more shots together. I was introduced to some of their friends from work, including a couple of cute girls. I think one was called Maggie, but I couldn't be sure. She talked about her job to me while I continued to imbibe. In another half hour I could barely stand on my feet and she had wandered off. I looked into the crowd from the bar and couldn't locate anyone, mostly because I couldn't keep the room from spinning. I sent Mack a text saying "left," stumbled outside, and managed to hail another cab. Somewhere along the way I told him to stop and I vomited out the window. Then, just like that, I was outside my apartment, which was odd because I didn't remember telling him my address.

With a great deal of effort I managed to extricate my heavy legs from the vehicle. I gave the cabbie a pair of bigger bills from my wallet, and, seeing that he seemed satisfied with the payment, I saluted him and haltingly made my way to the front door. For some reason I couldn't resist giving a glance to the night sky. It was a clear night, but only a few stars could be seen from my vantage point. The lights from the surrounding city muffled any others. Something about that struck me as tragic, but before a profound thought on the situation could take shape I tripped over the sidewalk and face-planted on my front lawn.

I tasted blood in my mouth. I spit once and then again, seeking to erase that disconcerting salty flavor from my gums. Failing to do so, I raised myself to my feet and shambled over to the house. Somehow opening the door, I stumbled through the hall and into my bedroom. There was only one thought on my mind now: getting to sleep. Once I fell asleep this day would be over and I would be safe. I threw myself onto my bed and half-heartedly covered up most of my frame with the blankets. I willed sleep to come, but the increasing pain emanating from my top lip blocked its arrival. So I lay there, head buzzing and face aching. Tears came unbidden to my eyes, welling up and spilling down my cheeks. I couldn't explain why I was crying, but I knew it wasn't because of the pain. Soon sobs wracked my body, like thunder following the lightning. I cried and cried, laying there as tears and blood mixed together on my pillowcase. Finally, exhausted, my body surrendered its consciousness.

11

DREAMSCAPE

I WAS STANDING on a beach. An endless beach, the sands extending into eternity. In the distance I could see the sun setting across the horizon, projecting its remaining rays across the shoreline. I turned around and saw my shadow stretching behind me, getting longer by the second. Then there were three other shadows, all stretched next to my own. I turned around and saw Mack, Finn, and Pete all standing next to me. They all wore bright, tranquil smiles and Pete was holding a Frisbee.

"Hey Muff, let's toss a little before it gets dark," Pete said. He flipped the disc towards me and took off down the beach. I threw it as hard as I could, and in the dusk I could barely see him extending for it. It grazed his fingertips as he dove. For an instant it seemed like he would make the catch, but the shock of his body hitting the sand jarred it loose. He lifted his head up from the sand and spit repeatedly, and after a couple of seconds his laughter traveled across the shore to my ears. Mack started running towards him and Pete lead him perfectly, making his heavy frame almost look graceful as he snagged the disc. After catching it Mack spun and threw it wildly over Finn's head towards the ocean. It didn't look like Finn had a chance at it, but we discounted his athleticism. He high-stepped his way through the shallows and somehow grabbed it without breaking stride. We continued like this for hours, the sun remaining halfway over the horizon throughout. I didn't question this;

I was grateful that the heavens would feel the need to assist us in the continuation of our fun.

Then, with a silent snap of invisible fingers, it was dark. It had been clear in the daylight, but looking up now I couldn't see a single star in the sky. Yet Pete, Mack, and Finn were all clearly visible, walking over to me across the sand. Pete tossed me a sweatshirt.

"Bundle up child, the sun's not with us anymore," he instructed. I looked at the sweatshirt and saw it was my old Fulton one, with orange letters printed across navy. I had lost it my senior year, but I knew without a doubt this was the original brought back to me. I threw it over my shoulders and saw my friends continue walking past me. Spinning, I finally noticed what had been supplying the light: there was a roaring bonfire in the distance. Music drifted over and I could make out the silhouettes of figures sitting and dancing around the blaze.

"Come on Muff, let's check out the scene down there," Pete said. "Maybe some cute ladies?" Facing away from the fire, his face was covered in shadow, but I could still make out the roguish smirk hinting that something wild would happen by the end of the night. We jogged to catch up with Mack and Finn, and before long we were in the midst of the strangers.

At first I would have guessed there were only about twenty of them, but I couldn't shake the feeling that there were others in the shadows. Unnerved by that prospect, I peered intently into the area beyond the fire but was unable to back up my initial gut feeling with any evidence.

They all looked up at the four new arrivals as we emerged from the darkness. I would guess their ages to be about equal to ours, which I just realized was probably about nineteen. I didn't know what I appeared as, but my three friends looked unmistakably younger, fresh-faced and projecting the eager enthusiasm of kids who know they have much left to experience. Our own excitement was mirrored in the faces of those around the fire. One, a tall handsome blond, stood up.

"Yo guys, you're more than welcome to share our fire and our beers. We got some pot too if you guys smoke. And s'mores, I can't forget the s'mores." He said all this with a confidence not quite befitting his apparent age, but I shook that off.

"Hey, thanks dude, sounds like a plan," Pete responded, looking at us as we smiled at the blond and his friends, half of whom were girls and all of whom were really attractive. However, as we advanced to the bonfire I hesitated for a half second. In that instant I felt sheer terror emanating throughout my entire body, freezing me in place. I couldn't explain it and wasn't sure I wanted to, but I knew right then something was horribly wrong. Pete sensed that I had stopped moving behind him and turned, giving me a quizzical stare.

"What's up Muff? Got a charlie horse or something? You look like you just peed your pants." Just like that, the moment passed as quickly as it had arrived and I felt foolish. And thirsty.

"Nah dude, it's nothing. Grab me a beer. I'm gonna try to talk to the tall brunette over there." I had seen this gorgeous female look at me briefly when we first showed up, and for some inexplicable reason I felt I had half a chance with her. Anything seemed possible tonight.

It didn't take very long to gather that this was an impressive group of people. They all had magnetic personalities and hilarious stories to tell. And it turned out I had guessed right about the brunette, whose name was Zoe. She did seem interested in me, and as the night stretched on I felt her hand brush against mine. I slipped my fingers in between hers and she gave me a dazzling smile.

"So what's the occasion for the party?" I asked her. It just hit me that we had talked about a million different things thus far but not about why any of these kids were here tonight. I knew she was from California, studied sociology at Colgate, and had an uncle that went to Fulton. I did not know what brought her to this wonderful beach.

"Oh. I think I used to remember, but now I can't." She frowned slightly and looked at the sand as if trying to recall, but seemed unable to make the necessary mental connections. She lightly shook her head and let that guileless grin return. "It doesn't matter, does it? We're both here and," she clasped my hand tighter, "that's all we need, right?"

I was inclined to agree. I felt lightheaded, but I suspected most of that was from the combination of pot and beer. My friends also looked very intoxicated, and I could see Mack twenty feet away trying to get two guys to jump over the fire with him. They were giving understanding smiles, but it was pretty clear they were not about to follow him into the flames.

As I brought my gaze back to Zoe's wonderful face I saw some movement out of the corner of my eye. Beyond the fire the darkness shifted slightly. Was I imagining things? No, I wasn't. There were other people out there where the light didn't reach. Why were they out there? This didn't make any sense. I asked Zoe if she saw them as well, but she just smiled and shrugged. Despite her nonchalant response, something went out of her when she heard me ask that question.

In the next half hour she would become more and more distant. Her eyes now seemed vacant; beautiful but empty. Increasingly, I wanted to be anywhere but where I was. I slipped my hand from hers, got to my feet, and swayed a little. I was drunker and higher than I thought. Shaking my head, I cleared it a little and began to weave towards Pete.

He was on the other end of the bonfire, and as I passed it I couldn't help noticing that its fires had died down considerably. In fact, it was now more coals than anything. The shadows began to close in, and it became clear that there were many people inhabiting them. Or at least I assumed they were people. I ran now, covering the remaining feet in a couple of seconds. I grabbed Pete and shook him hard.

"Dude, we have to get out of here right now. Things aren't...right." He looked at me through unfocused eyes and started to laugh.

"Muff, what are you tal..." I spun him around to face the dark. His eyes narrowed for a second and then got wide. He grabbed my shoulder. "Dude, what is going on?" He was now as terrified as I was.

"I don't know, but let's get Mack and Finn and get out of here." He nodded, horror etched in his face. A muffled roar echoed across the beach. The yell spoke of unimaginable pain, of agony unending, and we recognized the voice. It was Mack. We quickly scanned the lighted area, which was now only about twenty by twenty feet. Many of the partygoers had disappeared into the surrounding shadow, but this hadn't deterred the remaining kids from enjoying themselves. We couldn't see Mack, but in the darkness to our right I caught intensified movement. And multiple pairs of eyes. They looked human in shape, but glowed white. There were no pupils in these eyes, but I didn't doubt they saw me. I felt urine trickle down the side of my leg and something catch in my throat.

"Guys!" Finn stood a few feet away looking at us with the same dread in his wide eyes and trembling voice. Once Finn's yell echoed across the beach the other kids immediately stopped socializing. But they didn't look up at us or the surrounding dark, preferring instead to stare at the remaining coals. I saw a single tear roll down the cheek of the blond kid who had first invited us. With great effort he looked up at the three of us and said something so soft it was unintelligible.

"What?! What is happening?!" I screamed at him. I hated him so much. He had lured us here, had brought us into something beyond any of us. He moved his lips again and this time the words were just loud enough for the three of us to make out.

"They're not vampires. But it'll be better for you if you just pretend they are."

The music suddenly stopped and we could clearly make out a new set of sounds growing louder and louder in the darkness. It sounded like what was out there was feeding, and I could think of no noise more hellish.

"Finn, NO!" Pete screamed as our friend dashed off from what was left of the fire and into the dark. Finn was the fastest kid I had ever met, but it only took a few seconds after the darkness swallowed him before I heard him cry out. There was a brief silence, followed by more feeding sounds. I wish the fire still burned, if only so that I could light myself aflame and avoid whatever fate awaited me in the dark.

I felt a hand squeeze my arm roughly. Pete spun me towards him and we looked at each other. I felt rooted to the sand by my own terror, but in his eyes I saw dogged determination.

"Sam." He almost never called me Sam. "Sam, the beach is close. I can hear it. Run for the water with me. It's our only chance."

I nodded, and with a Herculean effort I moved my foot an inch. Just like that, my paralysis ended. We sprinted to the beach, and by our third step we were enveloped by the black night. I heard the sounds distinctly now, wheezes and the sounds of lips being licked. Something roughly grabbed my arm but I shook it off. Where it had touched lost all feeling. I kept on running.

"Sam!" Pete yelled to my left. I heard him grunt and a body hit the sand. "Run, Sam!" Then loud feeding noises. I ran even faster.

Suddenly I felt the sand turning moist, and soon after my feet were splashing frantically through the shallows. The maddening noise of the things in the shadows was quickly replaced by the roar of the waves ahead. I couldn't see them, but based on the sounds they made as they crashed against the beach they had to be enormous. I twisted my head around and saw the remaining light from the bonfire disappear. In its place were hundreds of pairs of bright white eyes. All staring into me. I turned back to face the invisible waves and felt the spray of the ocean sting my eyes. I was now up to my waist in the water, and as I continued to wade deeper I felt the water begin to pull me out to the sea. I sensed another wave forming not too far ahead, growing in size and sound as it careened towards me. I couldn't see anything, but still I reflexively closed my eyes. I could feel the wave coming closer and closer, its ferocity taking my breath away as its primal scream reverberated between my ears.

In that last second before I was engulfed, a strange thing happened. The overwhelming terror flowed out of my veins. In its place I felt a surge of gratitude. I was going to die here in the ocean's embrace. I didn't have to be afraid any longer. I didn't open my eyes, but I did smile.

"Thank you," I whispered.

Then I was awake in my bed. I had pissed my pants. My pillow was soaked with my tears and blood. I looked at my alarm clock. It was eight thirty, which meant I was going to be late for work. Today was April 13, 2007, and exactly one year ago Peter Hollis had taken his own life.

12
FALL AND RECOVERY

FOLLOWING OUR TRIP back from Fulton I was worried that Pete would slip back into the lethargic stupor which had defined his life beforehand. I was proven wrong as, almost immediately, his energy levels spiked. After what I had seen at Fulton I was wary, but chose to stay silent and fervently hoped the situation would somehow solve itself. Apparently what had beforehand been an occasional thing was now evolving into a persistent habit that he didn't see the need to hide.

I sometimes felt the pressing need to raise the issue, but when I considered how to bring it up I always came up empty. The most I managed to do was grill him about work one evening before Thanksgiving. He had gone out to the front stoop to smoke, a habit he had recently acquired, and although I didn't soberly enjoy cigarettes I asked for one as I sat down next to him. He gave me a curious look, but didn't refuse my request. We sat in silence for a few minutes, with him occasionally rubbing his nose. The nose rub had become a consistent nervous tic of his. I knew what it was from, and I also knew that he was aware of its visibility.

In front of us dead leaves drifted down the street, making soft brittle noises as they scraped against the concrete. They were being carried by the late fall wind, the same wind that forced me to wrap my arms around myself in a vain effort to keep warm. Pete seemed unaffected.

"So how was work today?" I hadn't asked him that question since his first few weeks at his job, both of us knowing the answer already. So it was with mild annoyance that he glanced over his shoulder at me.

"Fine." He took another long pull of his cigarette and slowly let the smoke exhale through his nostrils.

"Just fine? Is it actually fine? You don't seem thrilled when you come home." I was approaching uncharted territory here.

There was a long pause before he decided to humor me.

"Nope, I don't suppose it is actually fine. In fact, I might just actively hate it. My job and my life in general. Is that what you want to hear, Muff? That Boston's only redeeming quality is that I get to live with you guys?"

"Well, you can get another job."

"Do you like your job, Muff?" Shit. I should have seen this coming.

"Um, no."

"Then why don't you get another job? What's stopping you?"

I didn't want to provide an answer to this question, but unfortunately Pete supplied one for me.

"Is it because you think that it doesn't matter what job you have? That maybe one's as good as the other? That after a little while they're all going to make you feel a little dead inside? Or maybe it's just a little too much effort to try to shift gears? That you can't summon the energy to care?" He had now put out his cigarette and was looking directly into my eyes. I held his stare, refusing to back down.

"Maybe a little of all of those things. But I'm not you."

That elicited a laugh, one which echoed down the silent street. Pete's body shook with subsequent chuckles, eventually ending with a harsh cough.

"Thank god for that. I wouldn't dare wish that upon you." He raised himself to his feet and made his way back into the apartment, effectively ending the conversation. I stayed out on the porch for a couple more minutes and tried to think, but it was too cold. I retreated back inside to where he was cooking himself some more soup.

Pete didn't go home that Christmas, his first in Boston. Not only that, he didn't go to anyone's home for Christmas. Despite repeated offers from Mack, Finn, and me to stay over with our families (they all loved him, maybe as much as his own), he had waved us away. I remember seeing the saddened looks on Finn and Mack's faces as they left. They knew as well.

New Year's Eve was a blast, at least until Pete emerged from the bathroom with his nose bleeding. He didn't notice it at first, but upon being notified he was sufficiently mortified and let us know it would never happen again. A couple of weeks later his nose again started dripping blood on his shirt while he watched TV with me after work. He was less worried then. Just surprised and mildly embarrassed.

After the second nosebleed incident I was finally jolted into action. Pete clearly didn't care about his own health, so it was up to Mack, Finn, and me to care for him. Seeking to save him the embarrassment, I kept the intervention to just the four roommates. We let him know in no uncertain terms he would check into a drug treatment center and not leave until they were satisfied he was well on his way to recovery. I still remember the look he gave us. He had just used in his room, so he was already excitable, but he managed to keep still for about ten seconds as we sat around him in our living room. The last time we had all been like this, the three of us facing him, had been the previous summer when he had professed wanting to get a clean start. We still all believed he could redeem himself. Well, I still believed it. He gazed intently at Mack, who wouldn't look back, then at Finn, who coolly regarded him in kind. Finally, he let his searching eyes settle on me. I stared back hopefully.

"Fine." He almost had looked as though he was going to say something, but at the last second changed his mind. "I'll go. Thanks guys." He stood up, turned around, and went to his bedroom to pack his things. It was a surreal moment. I always wondered what he almost said, but never dared ask.

He took a two-week leave from work, preferring to use all his time off rather than utilize the company's drug treatment program. He told everyone he was going to visit some friends of his back in California. His family heard the same story just in case they called, which they hadn't done in months.

I visited him every day while he was there, Mack and Finn every other day. The first week he was a trembling, twitching mess. I would come into his room and I barely recognized his mannerisms. He looked like a man possessed, frantic and uncertain in his movements and speech. I had steeled myself, but it was still a shock. I knew Mack and Finn were seeing the same Pete as well, but back in the apartment none of us mentioned him once.

By the middle of the second week the worst was over. For the first time in a few months he had his body under his sway. Other than the occasional nose itch, it appeared his system had recovered. The staff there was extremely happy with his progress by the end of the second week, saying he had clearly communicated to them his understanding of the dangers of his previous situation as well as the necessary steps to avoid relapse. They were so impressed they allowed him leave a few days earlier than expected. There was nothing else they could do, they said. He appeared remarkably removed, both physically and mentally, from the fragile creature we had brought in. He, Mack, Finn and I all left the treatment center to the freezing embrace of a mid-February night, deep in the heart of a New England winter. Snow drifted lazily from above as we all crammed into Finn's car and shivered as he hurriedly tried to get it started.

"So, you ready to head back to work in a couple days, buddy?" Mack asked, leaning over from the back seat to pose the question to Pete. I had initially been really surprised his substance abuse hadn't had more of an impact on his work, but then I asked myself if I could do my job coked out of my mind. I decided I probably could and be seen as more of a go-getter in the process.

Pete paused for a second before answering. "No, I don't think I am. I had a lot of free time to examine my life while I was holed up at the clinic, and I don't think I am ready to head back to work. Ever."

Finn stopped trying to start the car and turned to his right.

"What do you mean, ever? Are you going to get another job?"

"No, I don't think I will. I think I could do without one of those."

Finn was silent. I just looked at the side of Pete's face as he stared ahead. He wasn't smiling. Mack was still leaning forward, his face next to Pete's ear.

"So, are you thinking of going back to school? You could definitely go back for philosophy. You'd make a great professor." Based on the eager smile planted on his face, Mack thought the world of this idea.

"Nah. I don't think more schooling is the answer. We did it already, you know? It was fantastic, but it's done. I'm ready to embrace reality."

Pete sounded both enthused and resigned at the same time. I didn't have the slightest idea what to make of him. I stayed quiet and let Finn ask the next question.

"So you don't want to work and you don't want to go to grad school? I'm not quite sure I understand what you're planning on doing with your life." Finn spoke a little more curtly than before. He always hated it when people got esoteric, and right then Pete was avoiding any categorization. Finn's life was rooted in a concrete understanding of where he was headed and what steps he had to take to get there. To stray from the path meant disaster, which is what he saw in store for Pete if he didn't alter his mindset.

Pete turned towards Finn, understanding in his face. He knew that Finn was scared, even more scared by the fact that Pete didn't appear the least bit worried. He reached out a hand and put it on Finn's shoulder as he turned behind and faced Mack and I. "Guys, I decided I'm going to write. Don't ask me about what, but I promise you that you'll appreciate it. I don't have a lot of money, but what I have will last long enough to write what I need to. There will be no more drugs, no more dulling the sharp corners of my life. Everything is crystal-clear now."

He smiled and I saw the old Pete Hollis, perpetually sure of himself. He knew what he was doing, and that was enough for me.

"Sounds good, dude," I heard myself say as I smiled back. Finn shook his head, not satisfied but giving Pete the benefit of the doubt. Mack shrugged, knowing that whatever was transpiring was beyond him. All he could do is be a safety net while Pete walked the tightrope. Finn finally started the car after a few more tries and we headed home, the silence inside mimicking the quiet of the winter night beyond.

*****

From the moment we got home that night, Pete was off and running. With the exception of meals and bathroom breaks, he was always in his room typing, the sound of his fingers rapidly hitting his laptop's keys echoing throughout the house. Mack, Finn and I were always on alert for any warning signs of a relapse, but none came. He seemed better than ever, perpetually glowing with excitement about whatever literary masterpiece he was penning. Deflecting our questions about his subject matter, he would instead ask us about our days and what was going on with us. In college Pete had always been exceptionally adept at giving incisive advice to his friends regarding any issues they might be having. He had a unique way of putting things in perspective, of lending some of his own inner clarity to those he spoke with. In the months since he had returned to us, that proactive Pete had rarely shown himself. I had almost forgotten he had existed, mired as he was in depression and substance abuse. But now he had returned, and instead of us worrying about him we found ourselves seeking his input.

As part of his rehab he stayed away from alcohol, but he would still go out with us for a few hours on either Friday or Saturday night. It was the only time he left the house other than for groceries and laundry. We would hang with old Fulton friends or go out to clubs to meet girls and Pete would tag along, smiling and cracking jokes. He happily served as my wingman during these winter months, getting me more females then than I had in the entire year and a half previous. He himself seemed uninterested in the opposite sex, despite repeated attempts from us and women to get him to reciprocate their interest. He said that with his writing he didn't have time to fool around with girls; they complicated things. The monk's life would suffice until the writing was done, he repeatedly informed us.

Interestingly enough, the only time I saw his rejuvenated veneer crack was when the news arrived, via Facebook, that Nora was in a relationship with some kid from Oxford. He visibly flinched when I entered his room and told him.

"For real?" he said softly, looking down at the floor.

"I mean, I asked Kristin Kilkowski, who goes to Oxford too, and she said they've been dating for a few months and it's kind of serious." It was a bit of a relief to see that these tidings cut deep; his recovery from the depths of despair and addiction had been too clean for my taste.

"Well, good for her. It's definitely been long enough since we were together and I would hate to think she was still stuck on me." He looked up and saw my critical stare. "I mean, I'm not psyched about it. I think I might still have had feelings even after all this time, but I'm sure I'll move beyond it as well before long."

"Good to hear. I just wish you would give the girls around here a shot at you. They're dying for a piece of Pete. Unless that's your plan—to make them want you so bad that they'll be fine with sharing you." I smiled and raised my eyebrows. He smiled back, but it was lacking any heart. He was just humoring me.

"Hmmm, how many girls at once do you think is overkill? Obviously two is fine, three can definitely work, and I guess I could see four happening, but don't you think people will just think I'm an asshole if I have five?"

"Only one way to find out."

"Yeah, I guess you're right, dude. Something to ponder before I head to bed tonight. Actually, I think I might do that right now. I got a lot of writing done today and I'll treat myself with a solid eight hours of sleep." Pete stretched as he said this, signaling for me to exit.

"You've really been plugging away for the last month," I said, seeking to gather any information about what exactly he was writing. "How many pages you got now?" I tried to peer over his laptop to maybe catch a sentence or two, but he deftly brought the screen down.

"It's not about the pages, Muff. But I'll say I think I'm about halfway through if my memory serves me right. Now get off to bed, you've got a big day of work tomorrow." He shooed me away with his hand.

"Fine. Sorry about Nora though. I haven't talked to Kate in a year and I still think about her sometimes." It was true. Maybe it was because the relationship was wrapped in the warm glow of college nostalgia, but I sometimes found myself wondering if she was the one. Oh well. Pete was right, I had a big company review tomorrow and I wanted to be well-rested. No falling asleep in meetings, or not at least until after the review.

"Love is tough stuff. Night, Muff," the words came out of Pete's mouth surprisingly subdued, and by the time I had answered in kind he had turned around and was setting his alarm. I turned around and left the room, closing the door behind me.

That night I couldn't get to sleep. Usually I passed out really easily, but the possibility of getting a negative review was really grating on me.

I realized it would actually feel worse than getting laid off, because my whole life I had only gotten positive reviews. I didn't give a rat's ass about this job, but I still wanted them to be proud of me.

Finally tired of tossing and turning, I got up and went to the kitchen and get some water. As I drank down its filtered goodness I heard something that made me pause. At first it sounded like coughing, but as I drifted closer I realized it was sobbing. My feet, following the sound, had taken me right outside Pete's door. The tortured sounds emerging from within were muffled but still obvious.

It made sense. He didn't want to admit it, but Nora's new relationship had taken its toll and he just wasn't willing to breakdown in front of me. Perfectly understandable. But the sounds of his misery...they were haunting. I felt shivers dance over my skin as I listened, unable to pull away. His pain seemed otherworldly, something emerging from the dark core of his being. It was completely at odds with the Pete we had been interacting with of late.

I didn't know what to do. It would be unbelievably awkward to barge in on a person when they were in that condition. I could just make things a lot worse. And maybe this was cathartic for him, a necessary release of bad mojo which was connected to Nora. As I quietly moved away from his door and back to my room, I told myself he would feel much better tomorrow.

I felt both vindicated and relieved when Pete did appear to be fine the next day and the following days. As winter began to draw to a close, he informed us he was making great progress on his writing. He suspected it might be completed in a few weeks, and when it was he wanted to go out big and celebrate with us. Drinks on him. I remember at that moment feeling, for the first time since Pete's return to us, admiration for him as I had in college. He had worked his ass off, forgoing not only the drugs which had threatened to consume him, but also any temptation to slip back into his previous self-hating malaise. In the depths of winter's darkness, alone in a room with just his thoughts, he had refused to focus on anything but his goal. Now he had almost achieved it.

It was that strength of will, especially now, that separated him from us. Finn might be dedicated and tireless, but he was genetically hardwired for industriousness. Pete, post-college, had found himself in a hostile situation drastically different from the one he had thrived in before. After a rough adjustment period he had shown himself as resourceful as ever, still an inspiration to those around him.

The tangible effects of his resurgence were felt in my own life. I continued to be disinterested in my work, but for the first time in a year I updated my resume and sent it to some companies that specialized in fields I might have some interest in. A few days later I heard back from one saying they wanted to interview me in a couple of weeks. As I finished reading their email a faint twinkling of hope blossomed in my breast. I sat back in my chair and smiled up at the ceiling, thinking that maybe happiness wasn't as far away as I had made it out to be. In the other room the sounds of Pete's furious typing could be heard, and I smiled even wider. I couldn't wait to read his magnum opus.

Fittingly, it was then that the first warm spell of the year arrived. It may have been the last week of March, but for a couple of days one could feel the temperate breezes of late May. We took advantage of it and managed to get four Fulton buddies to come play basketball with us at a nearby court. Everyone was rusty, but before long the warm temperatures eased into our creaking muscles and we remembered that we were still young. Bodies flew across the court as we sweated away the apathy of winter and savored the salty taste of our exertion. Mack, Finn, Pete, and I each had defined roles, carved out by years of playing with each other in Fulton's intramural league, and we immediately settled into them without much thought. Mack muscled his way down low, using his ample behind to clear out space and grab everything that came down from the rim. Pete, as the best ball handler and passer of the group, was the designated point guard. Finn utilized his lightning speed to slash towards the rim, and if there was an open three I was there to take it.

There are few substitutes for team chemistry in a typical pickup game of basketball. Success isn't dependent on your opponent as much as knowing the people you're playing with, and we knew each other's games like the backs of our hands. It really wasn't fair to the Fulton guys we were playing against, who never stood a chance despite being just as talented. Backdoor passes and great team defense, in addition to lights-out shooting by all four of us, had us winning the first four games by impressive margins. By the

time our fifth and final game was being played, two things were working
to even the playing field. The sun had set, making it hard for either team
to see the rim, and our buddies Tom, Ben, Johann, and Kyle were finally
gelling together as a unit. We had been down 8-4, but roared back to make
it 10-10. With the exception of Finn, everyone was exhausted, and even he
was noticeably winded. Pete was the worst off, struggling mightily to keep
up as we ran up and down the court. He had ravaged his cardiovascular
system over the previous months, and it was showing. I debated asking to
play half-court, because I knew he was too proud to request such a thing,
but I realized that that same pride would make him the most vocal critic
of that suggestion. Plus, he looked to be having a fantastic time, grinning
even as he bent over to catch his breath.

After a miss by Ben and a ferocious rebound by Mack, it was our
ball again. I took it up the court this time, but I could barely see it as
I dribbled so I dished to Pete. He flipped it up the court to Finn, who
didn't hesitate in taking it to the lane against both Johann and Kyle. For
a split second I thought he was going to launch an ill-advised lay-up and
hope to get the foul, but he thought better of it and passed it back to me
while he was still mid-air. The defense now was completely in disarray,
and right as Tom charged at me to prevent a game-winning shot from
beyond the arc I knew we had them. Mack charged down low and drew
coverage from Ben, which left Pete completely open. Without a second's
hesitation I threw the ball crosscourt to where he waited. He gathered it
up, measured the distance, checked to make sure his feet were behind the
line, and launched a two-pointer. You knew the instant it left his hands
it was good, and while no one could actually see the ball arc towards
to rim, the noise it made as it went through the net was unmistakable.
He pumped his fist as the other Fulton guys let their tired shoulders
slump. For them it was a frustrating loss, but just another game. For
us the symbolism was plain. He was better. Not completely healed, as
evidenced by him quickly lying down on the court to avoid passing out,
but better. We all ran up to him and slapped his chest and stomach as
he lay there. The smile he had had planted on his face the entire game
was still there, and he pumped his fist again in response to our slaps. We
waited a few more seconds and then pulled him back to his feet.

"You guys wanna go grab some beers with us tonight?" Ben asked as he wiped his face with his sweat-soaked shirt. Ben cracked me up. Short and stout, he was our resident lumberjack. The guy you would want with you in the woods, he had spent weeks on his own trekking throughout the American West. Flannel was his fabric, and as long as I had known him he had possessed a full red beard to match the hair on his head. The humor in this resided in the fact that his family was enormously wealthy. His dad was the CEO of Burger King or something, and none of us had any idea until we stopped by his house in Connecticut on our way down south for our senior year spring break. We followed his directions perfectly, but were still convinced he was playing a joke on us because the house we ended up at was palatial. The biggest house I had ever seen. Huge iron gates and a lawn the size of a football field containing gardens my mom would have killed to have. So we called him up to confirm. No, he said, he wasn't fucking with us, proving it by emerging from the mansion wearing nothing but a pair of Carhartts. We still laughed about him embarrassingly introducing us to his butler Gerard.

"Nah, dude...I've got more writing to do tonight...trying to get it done in a couple of weeks," Pete answered between labored breaths. Mack, Finn, and I nodded our heads understandingly. Pete had shown how much the writing had meant to him the last month, and we knew nothing was going to hold him back now. However, this was the first the other guys had heard of it.

"You're writing a book, dude?" Tom asked. He had known Pete from summer camp back in high school and had actually dated Nora before his friend. He seemed like the type of guy you would have expected Nora to be with, his easy-going nature reflected in his laid-back good looks. Dark, almost black hair, always looking a little mussed, rested above a delicately structured face that made Pete's look plain. And unlike Pete, Tom had done extremely well for himself since Fulton. So it was a testament to Pete's personality that Tom still looked up to his friend, visible respect in his face and voice when he asked the question regarding Pete's progress.

You could already see Pete anticipating the next question, because his smile became a little more forced. He hated being asked about the book's topic. We had held off any inquiries since he initially informed us, but that was because the only time we had seen him look vaguely upset in the last month was when he was asked about it. Tom didn't disappoint.

"Fiction? Non-fiction? What's it about?"

"Non-fiction. It's about the migration patterns of the Atlantic salmon and how global warming may be having a discernable impact on their ability to spawn effectively." Pete said this with the straightest of faces, and for an instant even I believed him. Tom and everyone else looked like they did as well. At a loss for words, Tom was bailed out by Pete, who let the smallest of smiles emerge on his face.

"The sequel will be even better. It'll be the Kama sutra of Atlantic salmon mating studies. Every position imaginable. Stuff you wouldn't want your kids to see."

The awkwardness broke as we all started laughing.

"Pete, you had me man. You really had me," Tom said as he shook his head sheepishly. "But seriously, what's the book about?"

"Seriously? Well, if you're serious, then I guess I'll have to let you know." Pete said somberly. "In a couple of weeks. Like everyone else."

"Not even a hint? A single bone to throw your anxious audience?"

"Hey, remember that time when you really wanted to have sex with Nora right after you two started dating freshman year?" Pete said all this without any anger and his candor clearly caught Tom off-guard.

"Um yeah, I remember that." Tom said, making uncertain eye contact with his friend.

"Yeah, well, when you two finally did it, it was fantastic, right? Earth-shattering? And that was after a couple of months of waiting."

Tom understandably looked shell-shocked. Everyone knew that he and Nora had been together before Pete and her, but no one had ever openly talked about it. Pete took his silence for a yes.

"Well, it'll be like that when you get to read what I wrote. And you'll only have to wait two weeks. The catch is that I won't give you hand jobs like Nora to tide you over until then. You'll have to tough it out." They were words spoken kindly, and Pete was smiling as he delivered them.

After a few seconds Tom smiled too. "Alright dude, whatever you say. Although I highly doubt what you wrote will be as amazing as young

Nora. They said she lost a step by the time you got to her." He smirked impetuously at Pete, who laughed loudly.

"They also say she lost the crabs by the time she got to me. But that's your problem, not mine," he shot back. "Alright, I'm gonna go. A pleasure playing with you guys. Let's make it a regular thing this summer. If it looks like you're giving it your all we might let up sometime in late August, just to reward your hard work." We all laughed at that, but we could see the other four guys would relish the chance to win after the day's sweep. At the hands of a recovering cokehead, no less.

We all shook hands and agreed to meet up later for drinks. When we left that night, we yelled goodbye to Pete from the hallway. We got a distracted "laters" from his room, quickly followed by more typing. The first round of shots that night were dedicated to Pete and his book, and when we got home at two in the morning he still was typing as quickly as ever. None of us disturbed him, but we all rested easier knowing he was leading a purpose-driven life.

13
ROUGH DAY IN THE RAT RACE

I SHOULD HAVE been rushing to get ready for work, but I wasn't. After I tossed my piss-stained sheets into my hamper and called in letting Legacy know I'd be late, I plodded over to the kitchen and poured myself a glass of orange juice. I drank it slowly, wincing at the stinging it brought my injured mouth. I knew I wouldn't be able to keep any food down so I didn't even attempt to consume any. Instead, I stared ahead at the wall in front of me and did my best to not consider my current situation. I didn't allow a single treacherous thought to pass between my ears, knowing that I would be fine as long as I was resistant to any introspection.

After ten minutes of engaging in this mental oblivion I felt safe enough to continue with my day. It took me a half hour to clean up both the house and my face. The trail I had taken to my room the previous night was clearly marked by the drops of blood. I always forgot how much people bled, even from the smallest of cuts. But I guess it could be worse. I stared at myself in the mirror, specifically at the gash and accompanying swelling on the left side of my upper lip. I looked as though I was sneering. That sneer accurately depicted how I felt facing my own reflection. I hated myself. What I saw was a shell, a skin-covered casing for a shadow. At that moment I couldn't give one concrete reason for my continued existence. On the other hand, I also couldn't generate any desire to end the pointless string of events composing my waking moments.

So I just abided. I was nothing more than a breathing vessel that contained a collection of memories and the basic lusts of life. They were what my soul subsisted off of. A critical truth, an insight which I thus far successfully suppressed, bubbled up to the surface. It exploded within my skull, showering my psyche with its knowledge.

I had arrived at a point in my life where I sought absolutely nothing from the future. I no longer had the slightest ambition or hope for myself, living only for whatever pleasures I assumed I could find in each day. That was the meat of my day, and I quenched my thirst for the spiritual not through my present life but through what I remembered of my past. And each year those memories grew weaker. My only solace lay not in the memories but in the understanding that I still desired the passion I had once possessed. If I felt it once, it was conceivable I could again.

In fact, I had felt the slightest tinge of passion yesterday when I had been talking to Lucie. Maybe there was a chance to expand on that tonight. Assuming she didn't mind that I was now mildly disfigured. I went down the hall, past Mack's snoring and Pete's empty room, to the front door where a note was taped. It was from Finn.

> *Saw some blood on the floor, assumed it was yours. Also, I'm*
> *assuming that piss on your bed is yours. Hope you're alright.*
> *I'll see you tonight and we can talk all about it.*
> *-Finn*

What was I going to talk to Finn about? That my life was unraveling? Nah. I crumbled up the note and made my way to my car, turned on both it and my iPod before I sped off into the post-rush hour traffic. Halfway through my commute I came to the conclusion that I was still drunk. Ignoring the dizziness and the subtle slowing of my reflexes, I weaved my way through traffic and cruised into the parking lot an hour and a half late. An attack of nausea struck me and I was forced to bend over the steering wheel. Eventually, after many deep breaths, the spell passed, allowing me to exit my car and head towards the building. I prayed I wouldn't vomit before I made it to the bathroom.

The first person I encountered when I entered was Beth, waiting at the elevator with a cup of coffee. I think she briefly debated pretending I didn't exist. Realizing this was an impossible task, she turned and smiled. The smile held no warmth, but despite that fact she still looked good. I hated her, but I was more repulsed by the fact I still found myself wanting what I saw.

"Are you just arriving, Sam?" At least she remembered my name. I had been facing forward towards the elevator, effectively hiding last night's wound, but I realized I couldn't mask it forever. I turned to face her and saw her blanch a little. She looked a little afraid. Maybe she assumed I got gotten in some bar fight.

"Yeah, I had a little accident last night. Slipped on my stairs and took a bit of a tumble." She didn't believe me and I didn't blame her. It was a flimsy story. I didn't have a staircase in my apartment. But I didn't care. The nausea was returning.

"Oh my god, it's great that you escaped with just that cut on your lip! You didn't have to go to the hospital, did you?" She said this in a concerned tone that an outsider might believe sincere.

"No, it's not big deal. I'll be fine. Just a little worse for the wear. Oh look, our elevator is here!" I pointed right as the bell went off and the doors opened. We both got on and rose up the first couple of floors in silence. Suddenly, she turned and faced me. I wasn't sure what I was expecting, but I had never seen anyone looked as enraged as she did at that moment. Reflexively, I stepped back against the wall of the elevator, hoping to get as far away from her as I could. Bile rose in the back of my throat and with a great deal of effort I swallowed it back down.

Her face contorted with fury, Beth took one step towards me and began whispering.

"I know you are telling everyone about what happened. I could see them looking at me in the halls when I walked around this morning. I know you didn't promise anything, but I can promise you I will never forget this. You will not ruin my career here with rumors and gossip." I flinched as she spat out that last syllable. My head, already aching from the night before, was now enduring an internal seismic shift.

I started to explain that I didn't say anything and that we had been seen together, but the look on her face said it all. She had just conducted an impromptu kangaroo court and, having pronounced me guilty, desired to see me hanged as soon as possible. I shut my mouth and felt its corners turn downward. Beth gave me one last malice-filled stare before composing herself and facing back towards the elevator doors. When they opened she purposefully strode out, giving a cheerful hello to our receptionist as she walked over to her office. No longer in her presence, the tension quickly left my body. Now I just felt worn out, exhausted to my core. Exposure to someone like Beth could really drain the life out of you.

I walked out and waved to the receptionist, careful to only show her the right side of my face. I knew if she saw my lip it would be a matter of minutes before most of the office knew. Donald had already taken a great deal of my anonymity away yesterday; I suspected by the end of today I would have little to none left. Things were disintegrating rapidly.

I made my way through the maze of cubicles without having to interact with anyone. However, I did encounter a word box. We had these word boxes scattered around the office, little gadgets some guys in tech had designed. Triggered by motion, they randomly generated phrases which flashed across their screens in sinister green letters. What unnerved me about these boxes was how ominous these "randomly" created combinations of words were. For example, today the word box I walked by, sensing my passing, flashed "Endless Void" across its little screen. Endless Void? Really? Random, my ass. These little boxes were mocking me and everyone else trapped in this corporate purgatory.

I resisted the urge to smash it and continued on to my cubicle. Starting my computer, I reached into my bag to grab my headphones. My hand pawed around without feeling their familiar shape, and in that instant a horrible realization dawned on me: I had left my headphones behind at the house. This was a bad situation, the severity of which was punctuated by the incessant typing from all the cubicles around me. I might go insane by the end of the day if I didn't drown out the sounds of my coworkers.

"Hi, Sam!" popped up on my screen. A message from Lucie. Maybe she could help me.

"Hey Lucie, you wouldn't happen to have any headphones I could borrow, would you?" I typed back. There was a pause, and then a response.

"Yeah, but you'd have to be a fan of bright pink."

"Works for me! I'll be over in a second," I quickly typed back.

As I made my way over to her cube my luck ran out. I ran into not one but three coworkers who I knew on the walk over, the last of which was Vice President Donald McLaughlin. I was astonished that I could have this many interactions with Donald in two days after months upon months of never crossing his path. I had managed to make my exchanges with my first two coworkers brief, mumbling something about accidents and continuing on my way, but Donald would not be so easily brushed aside.

"Sam, what happened to your lip!?" He didn't look concerned, but he did look surprised.

"It sounds silly, but I really did take a tumble down the stairs. The light in my house is at the bottom of the stairs, so I have to navigate them in the dark. I took a wrong step, slipped, and hit my mouth on the handrail. I suppose this will probably put a hiatus on my modeling career, right?" The joke elicited a chuckle from him, but it only lasted a second.

"I should think so. Well, it looks like you'll be playing catch-up for the rest of the day then. It's been a busy Friday. When I heard you would be in late I had Lucie handle the Hart outreach for their recent announcement. I'm sure she could use a little help with that, as she has already been taking care of the follow-up for the Voton release."

"Yes, I was actually just heading over there right now," I said, looking in the general direction of Lucie's cube in hopes of conveying the urgency of my journey across the office.

"You were? Well, that's great. I'm also going to need you to create an updated press list for Clearlake. It turns out there are some holes in our current one." This was disconcerting. Why was Donald giving me assignments? He apparently hadn't been kidding about taking a personal interest in my affairs. I nodded my head as he stared off into space.

"Well," he said, his face scrunching up as he thought. "That's all I have for now, but I'll let you know if there is anything else. Make sure to let Lucie know you're thankful for her helping you out." He turned away from me to look at his Blackberry, effectively ending the conversation.

"Will do, Donald." I said to his back. I was tempted to flip him off as well, but before I could give the notion any consideration another wave of nausea hit me. As my boss rapidly typed away I sped off to the bathroom on the other side of the office.

I just made it. Stumbling through the door and into the first stall I fell to my knees and immediately vomited in the toilet. Most of it made it in. Not bothering to close the door, I slid onto my side, closed my eyes to block out the painful light, and rested my head against the stall wall. Then my stomach convulsed and I puked again, barely getting my head over the side of the toilet bowl. Two more repetitions of that and my insides were empty. I wiped my mouth and unsteadily rose to my feet, glancing around for coworkers. There didn't appear to be any in the other stalls, but that moment Greg Shannon entered the men's room. Unaware of so many things in this life, Greg quickly put together my chalk-white appearance with the visible chunks of spew I had not cleaned up yet.

"Looks like someone had too much fun last night," he said as he chuckled. "Sam, you should know better!"

"Your mom should know better as well. But that didn't stop her from letting me do unspeakable things to her last night." I made my way over to the sink as Greg let out a mighty laugh.

"That's good stuff, Sam. That's good stuff!" he said as he pointed at me and made his way into the next stall. "Okay, I'm going to go use the facilities. You get better!"

Free of Greg and any troubling rumblings in my stomach, I turned my thoughts to Lucie. I was determined not to be caught off-guard again when I visited her. I exited the bathroom and briskly walked back across the office. I stopped short of her cubicle, where I spent twenty seconds thinking of a serviceable opening line, finally settling on something relating to me winning a boxing championship last night. I quietly maneuvered my way around to where her cubicle wall ended and poked my head in.

She had already spun her chair around and was facing the exact spot where I had emerged. Shit. She must have sensed me somehow.

Maybe I had been breathing heavily? She looked frazzled, worn down from the added responsibilities that had been assigned to her in my absence. Her laptop had countless windows open on it, and around it lay scattered papers covered in red revisions. But that didn't stop her eyes from twinkling as she directed an amused smirk at my fat lip.

"Oh crap, did I miss the fight last night? Was it on HBO? I don't get HBO," she said. She stole my line. Once again I lacked any witty comeback.

"Ummm, yeah. You don't look very surprised."

"Word travels fast around the office. And with this thing called the Internet, you don't have to worry about people overhearing you gossip. It's great!"

I laughed, but was surprised to see her cocky smile falter for an instant.

"So...we still on for tonight? Or do you need time to heal?" She said this in a way that could be understood as her being either snarky or unsure. I took it as a little of both. Lucie was somehow able to project both vulnerability and confidence interchangeably.

"I don't think any amount of healing I do today will make me look presentable, but if you still want to go have some fun then, yeah, we're definitely still on." I gave a big smile and winced when it stretched my lip.

"Okay, great! However, your late arrival gave me plenty to keep busy for the rest of the day and through the weekend, so if you want to actually see me tonight you're going to have to let me get back to it." She winked and spun around back to her desk, immediately setting her brainwaves back into work mode. I saw all my coworkers do it when they needed to buckle down for an extended period of time. No smiles, no jokes, no emotion, just a lot of frenetic typing and clicking for hours on end. I had yet to try it.

It just didn't seem like a lot of fun. I remember being intense when writing papers at school, but that was because the topic was interesting or it was due in an hour and I had six pages left to produce. A very different scenario than trying to arrange outreach for an announcement by some company I couldn't give two shits about. But maybe I could try it today to help Lucie out.

"Yo, I'll take over the rest of the Hart outreach if you don't mind. Donald suggested as much." She stopped briefly and gave me grateful glance over her shoulder.

"Really, Sam? That'd be a huge help."

"Hey, might as well do some work while I'm here right? I can always watch my YouTube videos later."

Lucie once again understood I wasn't lying, but didn't act annoyed as she handed all the Hart materials over to me.

"Okay, you can be the guy who screens them for me. Send me over the cream of the crop, and when I have a free moment maybe I can squeeze a laugh in. Just don't give me any half-assed Jackass-style shit. I only want the best. You got that, Orcutt?" She said this without even a hint of humor in her voice.

"You got it, Miss Mallory!" I saluted her as I took the Hart materials and marched out of her cube. I smiled the entire walk back, ignoring the ogling eyes of the coworkers I passed on my way.

*****

I made it almost two hours in "work-mode" before I finally indulged in some non-work emailing. First, I had to fend off multiple emails from Greg, who insisted on hearing some more details on the Beth situation. He apparently was fascinated by me and my "exploits." Why couldn't they transfer this guy to Cleveland or something?

Once I stonewalled him I got in an entertaining "would you rather?" email chain with Meg and Henry. It concluded with both Kate and I deciding we would rather sneeze fire ants than have a gigantic unicorn horn protruding from our foreheads, with Henry vigorously defending that preferable nature of the latter.

After a half hour of not doing anything work-related, I figured it was about time to try to finish up the Hart outreach. For Lucie's sake. But before I did I wanted to sound off quickly on my boy Donald. I knew my buddy Dan had worked with him on a couple of teams when Donald was still just a manager and I wanted his opinion. So I penned the following email:

Yo dude,

Sam here. Doing some Hart stuff for Donald, who seems to have taken a specific interest in me. You had him as an immediate boss…was he always a complete douche bag then? Cause this guy seems determined to suck as much as he possibly can. One of those guys who can't wait to shit just to show you how it doesn't stink. Between him and Beth I'm pretty sure this company has enough hot air to travel the world in a balloon. But yeah, your thoughts?

I hit send.

You hear of it happening all the time. People send hundreds of emails everyday, and sometimes the addresses in an email are not looked carefully at before the "send" button is hit. In my experience, the most common mistake is to make a Freudian slip and put in the address of the person you are talking about rather than the person you mean to send the email too. Of course, this is often the most devastating mistake, as virulent messages go right to the individual or individuals you were directing your hateful thoughts at.

I had close calls before. This wasn't a close call. I realized right after I hit "send" that the name in the "to" box wasn't "Dan Killington." It was "Donald McLaughlin."

And, just like that, I was completely fucked. I couldn't cancel it, but I could stare at my screen, mouth agape. After about five minutes of doing that an automated reply email popped up in my inbox from Donald's computer. It read:

Hello, I'm going to be out of the office from now until Monday, April 16. If you need further assistance don't hesitate to contact our receptionist at extension 4200.

Sorry for any inconvenience,
Donald McLaughlin
Executive Vice-President
Legacy Communications
dmclaughlin@legacy.com

"We have nothing to fear but fear itself"
-Franklin Delano Roosevelt

So he had left early for the weekend. I popped up from my cubicle to get a look over at his corner office. It was dark and almost certainly was locked. I walked over as casually as I could, glanced around to make sure no other sets of eyes were witnessing, and yanked on his door handle. It *was* locked.

"Shit!" I said, loudly enough for multiple heads to pop up from their cubicles. Like a bunch of prairie dogs. I apologized and made my way back to my own cube. When I sat down two revelations came to me.

The first was:

Donald has probably already seen this email on his Blackberry. And when he comes in on Monday, he will have you fired. Beth will encourage it. Your time here is over.

The second was:

Why should you fucking care?

After that I felt much better. Well, a little better. It was still a bit of a shock, as I had been here for over two years. That's a lifetime for a twenty-four-year-old. But I could cope. I spent the rest of the afternoon emailing with my friends and making sure the Hart materials were perfect for Lucie. I didn't let any of them know what I expected would happen to me on Monday, if only because it would kill the exuberant Friday mood that always hit around four. At five I walked over to Lucie's desk and dropped off the Hart materials. She was at a meeting, so I made sure to put a post-it note on them with the message "Tonight, Tonight" on it.

As I waved goodbye to the receptionist it struck me that this was it. It wasn't like I didn't hate this job, but it just seemed so sudden. Even though I could have predicted my leaving this job in a million different ways, this particular ending had caught me by surprise. Then it hit me. Today *was* Friday the Thirteenth. I laughed out loud as the elevator doors closed on me and my life at Legacy Communications.

14

NO ONE GETS THROUGH THIS LIFE UNSCATHED

WEDNESDAY, APRIL 12, 2006. That day it wasn't my alarm that woke me up, but rather the smell of spring drifting in through my open windows. I lay in bed inhaling and exhaling, savoring every breath. It was almost ten o'clock, which is when I had set my alarm. I had taken the day off from work to prepare for and then have my interview downtown. My preparation, as I had planned it, would consist of sleeping in until ten, ironing my only suit, and getting on the subway for the half-hour trip to my prospective new employer's impressive high rise.

I had woken up ten minutes early and wasn't going to let it go to waste. I was going to breathe for all I was worth until that familiar beeping sounded. When it finally did I felt like an eternity had passed, a blissful time where only my sunlit room existed. I climbed out of bed, exited my room, and made my way over to the kitchen to enjoy a leisurely breakfast.

Before I could grab the cereal of my choice I remembered I had company. Joining the birds in their morning song were Pete's fingers, making loud tapping noises from his room. It was the only tangible sign he was alive. None of us had seen him since Sunday, when he had commanded no one bother him unless the circumstances were truly dire. He hoped that by the middle of the week he would be finished, but until then he would be distracted by nothing. I had no idea what he had been eating; all his groceries had disappeared last weekend.

My own stomach ached, forcing me to stop pondering Pete's progress. I crouched by the cereal cabinet and opened the door, but before I could grab my Cocoa Puffs a mighty roar of "YES!" erupted from within Pete's room. I paused, my hand still extended towards the cereal box, unsure what course to take. I debated calling out and asking if everything was okay, but the dilemma became moot as he burst through his door into the kitchen.

Fist raised in triumph, he surveyed both the kitchen and me as a conquering hero would. He looked like hell, sporting a week's worth of stubble over a pale, drawn face. Yet his aura struck me as powerfully reminiscent of the last night before graduation. During his impromptu speech that night he had seemed more than human. He had appeared as a living embodiment of hope, brimming with a confidence that couldn't be critiqued. It was now as it was then. It didn't matter how small this accomplishment was in the grand scheme of things, just as it wasn't important that our graduating from a small New England college went largely unnoticed by the outside world. You took one look at the passion flowing from Pete and you didn't question. You couldn't question.

So I returned the smile he had planted on his face. Eventually the initial surge of emotion passed and he slowly lowered his fist.

He continued to stand there, appearing to still be trying to grasp his recent accomplishment. That or he was so exhausted he couldn't think anymore. He was looking at me, but I could tell he wasn't really seeing me. I gave him a few more seconds and his eyes regained their focus.

"Muff, I did it. I finished." The words tumbled out of a parched mouth, his voice croaking from disuse.

"That is awesome, dude, I'm real proud of you," I said, genuinely moved seeing Pete taste success again. I rose to my feet and walked across the room, arms outstretched. "Come on buddy, bring it in. You deserve it." My smelly friend walked into the hug waiting for him, returning it in kind. When he pulled apart he tried unsuccessfully to shake the cobwebs out of his head.

"Yeah. I did it. That's that. And tonight we'll celebrate. But right now I'm going to go sleep until dinnertime. See you then!" Still intoxicated on his own euphoria, he waved goodbye to me and walked back into his room. The door closed, and after a couple of seconds I heard the bed springs groan as his body collapsed onto the mattress.

As I ate my cereal, my thoughts drifted ahead to my interview. I realized that I sincerely wanted to get this job and match Pete's personal achievement with one of my own. If Pete could move beyond the shadow of Fulton and challenge himself then so could I.

I left the house that day knowing I would ace the interview. When I returned I had done just that. Now our apartment would have two reasons to celebrate tonight.

*****

When Pete emerged from his room it was almost seven. Mack, Finn, and I had been drinking since six and had called all our friends in the Greater Boston area letting them know we were going out big that night. It being a Wednesday, we hadn't expected much of a response, but almost three-fourths of those we called said they would love to go out in honor of Pete's accomplishment. Word had spread regarding his writing and apparently we were not the only ones who were rooting for our roommate to succeed.

Towel over his shoulder as he prepared to take a much-needed shower, Pete first popped his head into the living room. We had just finished another toast in honor of the new author, and, sensing his presence, we all turned and immediately gave another.

"To Pete!" we roared, crashing our bottles together. Shockingly, the look on his face was anything but happy. The first word that came to my mind was "haunted." Before I could analyze where his earlier exuberance had gone, he took an elaborate bow. When he popped back up his face glowed with happiness.

"Thank you, gentlemen. I see Muff has ruined the surprise for you both, but that's understandable. Yo, toss me one of those beers. I'm feeling mighty thirsty."

Mack obliged him, throwing a bottle across the room. Pete adeptly snagged it out of the air. "Thanks, dude. I'm going to drink this in the shower, and when I come out I want you guys to be ready to go. Cool?"

We all cheered his name again and he grinned. "I'll take that as a yes." He took a swig and walked off to the bathroom as we finished our beers and opened others. The night already had the vibe of a memorable one.

When Pete emerged clean-shaven and hygienic a half hour later, there were only two beers left. We demanded he drink them before we all went out and he agreed. While he drank we peppered him with questions.

"So do you have any connections in publishing?" Finn asked.

Pete held the bottle to his lips as he appeared to consider this question.

"No, I don't believe I do."

Looking a bit bemused, Finn hesitantly put forth his follow-up question.

"You are going to try and get it published, right? Cause I know a few people you might want to talk to."

Pete took a substantial gulp, swallowed, and looked at Finn. He appeared ready to say something before reconsidering. Muffling a burp in his hand, he smiled benignly.

"Yeah, I'm sure I will try to get it published. I just don't want to think about that right now, you know? We'll talk about meeting up with your friends tomorrow."

This answer seemed to satisfy Finn, who nodded his head approvingly.

"When can we read it?" Mack blurted out. "Is it fiction? Are we in it?"

"Tomorrow. Non-fiction. Yes, you're all in it."

"We're all in it? Is it like a memoir?" I asked, slurring my words just the slightest. I hadn't had any dinner and the beers were catching up with me.

"Like I said, you can read it tomorrow and all will be made clear," Pete said distractedly as he finished the second of his beers. I didn't know why he was being so evasive, but whatever the issue was it would reveal itself tomorrow. The combination of intoxication and excitement easily subdued any feelings of unease. I was ready to party. I stood up and faced Pete.

"Okay then, how about heading downtown to the Attic? That place is always happening." This was true, which is why Mack, Finn, and I had told everyone to meet up there at nine. It was already eight thirty.

"Sounds good to me," Pete said as he got up from his chair. "I'll let you guys know ahead of time that I plan on drinking you all under the table tonight. So you might just want to call in sick to work right now."

Mack walked over and put an arm around him. He had already had at least six beers but hadn't shown any hint of drunkenness.

"Buddy, that's sweet of you to say, but I just don't think that's going to happen for two reasons. First, there is no world that exists where you could ever out-drink me. Second, I quit my temp job today so I wasn't going to work tomorrow anyway. But hey, give it your best shot!"

Pete's eyes glittered. "Is that a challenge, Francis?"

Mack gave an exaggerated sigh. "I think writing a book has gone to your head. Let's go!"

It was a fifteen minute walk to the subway and it started to rain almost immediately after we left the house. However, this rain, unlike similar precipitation a month ago, carried with it the taste of spring, so instead of going back for umbrellas we sprinted and savored the droplets as they smacked into our faces. Once at the station we sped down the escalators and saw a train just about to leave. Finn was naturally the first in, and the doors were beginning to close when Pete and I launched ourselves through. Huffing and puffing, Mack reached the train and jumped towards the door headfirst. Only his head would succeed in making it into the car. The doors closed in on it, he swore loudly, and they reopened again. As he stumbled into the car a bunch of younger girls sitting at the end of the car giggled loudly. He gave them an enthusiastic wave and plopped down next to us. We were all soaked but couldn't stop smiling.

"Thanks for waiting up, guys," he said accusingly.

Pete took Mack's meaty paw into his own.

"Hey, Mack, we have faith in you. We never would have gotten on this train if we thought you couldn't make it. Now go talk to those girls. You've made quite an impression on them." To emphasize his point he gestured to where Mack's admirers sat. Mack peered at them, saw a couple females he liked, and ambled over, making sure to drag Finn along with him. If Mack had one great strength as a person, it was a complete lack of shame. As they approached the girls Finn apparently saw one to his liking, because he shook off Mack's hand and assumed his typical nonchalant stride. We both smiled at the young romance unfolding, but Pete's didn't last long. He turned to me.

"How'd that interview go today?"

"I could be wrong, but I think I aced it. My time at Legacy might have come to an end." The acknowledgement of this made me tingle with excitement. I had finally taken initiative in my life and, no matter how it turned, out I was proud of myself.

"That's great, dude, that's really awesome." Pete's grin came back, but it was melancholy. He put an arm around my shoulder and directed his gaze towards Mack and Finn. "You know, I've been worried about you. Finn's always moved forward like his ass is on fire and Mack is protected from the harsh reality of life. But you're more like me. We're..." He paused and looked down at his feet. "I know life isn't going to be easy for you. I wonder if college crippled our survival instincts. But knowing you're moving forward and not taking what life gives you, that puts my heart at ease. Just keep that aggressive mindset and I think you'll be fine. Don't get caught up in the past and don't ever think the best has already passed you by. Because it hasn't. You have great things ahead of you. Just keep your eyes ahead so you can see them, alright?" He looked up at me, his face a contradiction to his hopeful words. He appeared pained, like he was going to vomit.

"You okay, Pete?" I tentatively asked. "You only had a few beers. I know it's been a while, but come on, shape up." I just wanted him to be okay. In my head I screamed at him to be okay. He had written a goddamned book! He should be fine. Why wasn't he fine?

"Me?" he asked, more to himself than me. He appeared to give it some thought and grimaced. "Yeah, I'm fine." He paused before looking back over at our roomies. "Mack and Finn seem to making inroads. Let's join them." Quickly rising, he sauntered over to the pair and the half dozen girls they were conversing with. Shaken by Pete's latest batch of erratic behavior, I waited a few seconds and then followed suit.

It turned out these girls were headed to the Attic as well, and we all streamed out from the subway station onto the street laughing and talking like we had nothing to lose. Pete and I had been conversing with these two girls Alli and Andrea, cute undergrads who appreciated the age gap between us. Naturally, Pete and I exploited our unknown "adult" lives. He was the aspiring author who had just completed his first work and I was on the corporate fast track to success. These narratives were consumed by the girls with relish. They eagerly asked us questions about our jobs and lives, to which we gave answers which stretched the truth as much as we felt feasible.

As it was a Wednesday, the streets were largely silent, the notable exception being the Attic. As we approached the sounds of merriment drifted out, and Mack, Finn, and I assumed that at least a few of those patrons were Fulton grads waiting for Pete's arrival. Our suspicions were confirmed when our group entered.

"Pete! Pete! Pete!" chanted a crowd of about twenty in the back of the bar. They looked to have had enjoyed themselves in the time up to Pete's arrival and now were pleased to turn their admiring eyes towards the man of the hour. The man himself seemed touched by this impromptu celebration in his honor. Pete looked downright shy, blushing slightly as he raised a hand in acknowledgement of his friends.

Our friend Tom emerged from the group and tossed an arm around Pete. His face was as flushed as Pete's, but it wasn't from embarrassment.

"Hey, buddy, I knew you could do it! Congrats! Since I suspected you and Nora weren't talking, I gave her a call a couple of weeks ago and let her know you were close. She says she's so proud of you."

"Thanks, Tom. That means a lot. What drink you got there in your hand? Well let's get me and everyone else here one of those." Pete led us all over to the bar and then yelled out to our assembled friends. "Shots of tequila on me! Everyone gather round!" Cries of discontent arose from our ranks. We had been expecting to buy the new author his drinks. Holding his hands in the air Pete hushed us. "First round on me! Then Mack's buying for the rest of the night!"

Mack looked up from the girl he had been talking to with a bewildered expression on his face, eliciting a roar of laughter from the crowd.

Pete opened his wallet after a couple dozen shots had been poured and pulled out several twenties he had nestled in there. I had been amazed he even had the money to buy us all shots, but apparently he still had a bit of a nest-egg. He saw me staring open-mouthed and gave a sardonic grin.

"Well, Muff, that's the last of it," he said as he pushed the money to the bartender.

"Of what?"

"My money. That's all I have left. And if you ask me, what a wonderful way to spend the rest of it." He pressed a shot glass into my open palm and placed a lime in my other hand.

I was stunned, and the uneasy feeling I had felt earlier on the subway came back with sudden force. Before I could say anything, Pete raised his glass high and everyone crowded in to hear.

"Thank you, everyone, for coming out on this special hump day!" he said as he turned to face the semicircle of people surrounding him. "I'm a happy man right now. Not because I finished my book, but because I have all of you to celebrate its completion with."

"Yes! Go us!" Tom yelled from the back of the crowd. Pete acknowledged him with his glass and continued.

"Yep. It's great to know that even a couple of years after graduation everyone is still tight. As the years go on it's going to be easier and easier to lose touch. You'll be caught up in your own lives and your own careers, and the draw of old college friends just won't seem as powerful. In expectation of this drift I ask you all one favor. Remember tonight. Remember how great it is to spend time with each other, old friends from a time when the future seemed limitless." I tossed an arm around him.

"College! Woooooooooo!" I yelled, and it came out more sarcastic than I intended. He looked over at me, laughed, and collected his thoughts again.

"Exactly. We all became who we are today then, and let's never forget those who were with us when that happened." He paused and considered his raised glass. "Now for the toast!" We all raised our glasses a little higher. "To Mack!" he bellowed across the bar. Mack once again looked confused as everyone laughed.

"To Mack!" we answered as we downed our shots.

Mack bought the next round as the night quickly escalated. Some of us hadn't seen each other in many months, but no one wasted time bringing their old classmates up to speed with their lives. We were all together and that's all that mattered. After everyone had congratulated

Pete different groups splintered off, but the largest still remained around the new author.

"So when are we going to get to read it?" a friend of ours named Liz asked. A cute little blonde and the object of many Fulton's boys' affections, it was well known she always had a special thing for Pete. Now she was trying to sound mildly interested, but the eagerness in her voice betrayed her carefully maintained detached demeanor.

"How's tomorrow sound?" Pete answered. "It's there in my computer, and I printed out and bound one personalized copy for my roommates here." He gestured to us. "I figure they put up with me all this time, they deserve to have the first peek at what's inside."

"And don't worry, Liz, if it's crap we'll make sure it'll never see the light of day," Finn assured her. That earned a raised middle finger from Pete.

"You wrote it in just a couple months?" This question came from a kid named Adam, a Harvard graduate and friend of Finn's from high school. I had the misfortune of meeting him once we all moved to Boston. The epitome of an entitled prick, his success post-college (he was in finance or something, I could never remember) had only further fueled his arrogance. I knew Pete felt similarly, but he would never show it.

"Hey, Adam! Didn't see you there buddy. Yeah, just a couple months. Really devoted myself to it."

"And you managed to do this while working?" Adam was incredulous.

"Nope. I quit my job before I dived into the writing. Not enough time for both. But it's not like I'm hurting for money. In fact, let me buy you a drink!" He put down his credit card to pay, throwing an arm around Adam and asking how the world of finance was treating him.

As they talked I wandered off to the bathroom. During my piss I tried to focus on exactly what was bothering me. I had stayed quiet since the toast, unable to shake the knot in my stomach despite the ample amount of alcohol I was consuming. Outside, I heard a series of yells, each louder than its predecessor. It seemed everyone was following Pete's generous example and the gathering was rapidly turning sloppy.

Was Pete actually broke? Was I missing something about him, some warning sign to tip me off that things were not copasetic? After that first round had been bought I had been trying to spot something off, an effort that was proving more and more difficult as my brain cells died en masse. I'm sure I had looked absurd, squinting at Pete across the bar, but some part of me refused to let it go. He seemed great, chatting up old friends and making new ones. I finished my business in the bathroom and wandered back to the bar, and the first thing I saw was Pete putting a girl's number into his phone as he smiled at her. I couldn't pinpoint anything worrisome about his behavior.

Except for one thing. After that first group shot, Pete had been bought the beer he currently held in his hand. It had been over an hour and he still nursed that one, solitary beer. He was staying sober. This was his party, his moment to cut loose from the strain of the last couple of months, and he was refusing more drinks from his friends. I understood that the impact of his past drug use could very well be influencing his decision to maintain control, but it wasn't. Never once had I or anyone else around Pete suspected that he would relapse into chemical dependency. He had allowed drugs into his life, and it was obvious the moment he departed the clinic that he was finished with them. Since then it had been only smooth sailing, and I refused to believe it was any different on this night. Something else was transpiring here. I pulled my half-finished beer from my lips and slid it down the bar. No more drinking for me tonight.

I walked over to where Pete stood talking and threw my arm over his shoulders. He turned and, seeing it was me, gave me a smile and clapped me on the back.

"How we doing, Muff? Seeing anything you like?" He gestured at the girls scattered about the bar. "This is your big night too, go nuts!"

"Nah, I'm pacing myself right now. What did I interrupt?" I looked around at the circle of happy faces.

"Well, my man, we were just discussing the time Ben hooked up with my favorite cousin when she visited Fulton our junior year. You remember that, don't you?"

I laughed and glanced over to where a bashful Ben refused to make eye contact. Pete's cousin Emily had visited as a pre-frosh and she and Ben had ended up drunk in his bed. When Pete found out that night he wasted no time. While they slept, their clothes scattered all over the floor,

Pete snuck in and proceeded to take a silent, neat dump in Ben's boxers. To this day Emily still believed, against Ben's fervent denials, that he had profound case of incontinence.

"If I remember correctly, you hooked up with Tom's sister freshman year," Ben shot back. Now everyone brought their amused gazes back to Pete, interested to hear his take on this.

Pete looked thoughtful for a second, fingers stroking his chin as he glanced over to where Tom was talking with a girl across the bar.

"You're right, Ben. I did. But she was twenty-five and I was eighteen. Nothing wrong with that in my book. However, I don't know if I ever told you the whole story about that night…"

*****

It was past midnight when we exited The Attic. Now Thursday morning was upon us, and the realization of that had brought a rapid end to the merrymaking. Our time in there had passed surprisingly fast for me, especially since I hadn't been drinking for the last couple of hours. I felt the brisk night air sweep away most of the remaining buzz from my brain and I glanced around at the assembled group, the large majority of which were extremely drunk. While our friends loved to have a good time, I wouldn't have expected this many of them to readily embrace the hangovers they knew they would be enduring at work the next day. But I understood why. If I hadn't had my misgivings about Pete I would have been the drunkest of them all right now—except for maybe Mack, who could presently be heard vomiting in a nearby alley. He had been the lucky recipient of any drinks declined by Pete.

Pete, who had maintained his sobriety for the remainder of our time in the bar, had his arms around Tom and Liz, giving the impression that they were holding up the intoxicated middleman. One look at their faces made it clear the opposite was true. Pete let go of both to go check on Mack, causing them to slump into each other and a nearby streetlight. Then they started sloppily making out.

"Yo, let's catch the T!" The words were bellowed from behind me by Finn, who was the most hammered I had seen him since college. I jumped despite myself, and when he saw he had scared me he laughed and tried to pick me up. The end result of this was him tripping over the street curb and laying out hard on his back. He groaned in pain before joining the laughter of those who had seen him fall.

Some friends hailed cabs to bring them home, including Tom and Liz, who only stopped making out long enough to tell the cabbie the directions to Tom's house. The rest of us would all be taking the subway home. Before I could yell at Pete and Mack to hurry up, they both emerged from the alley. Mack's shirt was covered in puke, but he smiled wearily as Pete's hand raised his own into the air.

"He's all better, everyone! Just ate some bad seafood for dinner! Right Mack?" Pete turned his face to Mack, who nodded his head. "Like I said, he's all better!" We all broke out into scattered applause for the rejuvenated Mack, who responded by jogging awkwardly ahead to the nearest subway station, motioning for us to follow him down.

The group all began to file down the stairs, but before I could descend to the tracks below I felt a hand on my shoulder pulling me back. It was Pete.

"Hey buddy, can I talk to you for a second? I don't know why you decided to stay sober, but I'm glad there are two of us." He made brief eye contact with me before glancing up at the sky. I felt rumbling beneath us. The subway.

"Train's here!" I heard Finn yell from below.

"We'll catch the next one!" Pete called back. His whole body was shaking, but he closed his eyes and it stopped. I pretended not to notice, waiting for him to speak. After an awkward quiet, it was clear I would have to break the ice.

"Pete, man, what's up? Why didn't you drink like everyone else? The only reason I didn't was because of you. This is your big night. You should be celebrating!"

He looked back at me ruefully. "Sam, I *was* celebrating tonight. It was fantastic seeing everyone, and on a big night like this I just wanted to be able to sit back and appreciate it all. Let it all sink in one more time and remind myself what a great life I've had."

That made sense. "Okay, your call. Nothing wrong with a sober night. And Mack might have choked on his own puke if it wasn't for you." We both smiled, but the smiles faltered when we wondered if Mack might in fact die that very way. Then Pete's disappeared completely.

"Look, Sam, I just wanted to let you know that it's been a blast being your friend all these years. We've been through so much, and you've never let me down. I love you, man." I didn't have a quick answer to those heartfelt words, but I don't think Pete expected any. He wrapped me up in bear hug, held it for a couple of seconds, and clapped me on the back as he pulled away.

"So, are we supposed to start making out now?" I asked, bringing my face closer to his. He laughed without humor and pushed me back.

"Funny, dude, real funny. Just thought I would put that out there." He sniffed and I looked at him closer in the dim streetlight. There were tears in his eyes. And I didn't think they were happy tears.

"Pete, what is wrong?!" I screamed at him. "God dammit, tell me what is the matter! I'm scared, man!" This entire night he had been altering between transcendent inner peace and tortured despair. Now I was determined that he provide some explanation. There was a long silence, me looking at Pete and Pete looking at the pavement in front of him.

He blinked, a couple wet streaks running down his cheeks. "If I could explain it, then I could fix it. But I can't." He gestured around us at the hushed city streets. "This just isn't right. Nothing is right!" Pete screamed the last word, his voice reverberating into the cloudy night sky.

I had no answer to all of this. He continued.

"I wish I had regrets. But I have no regrets. I've been blessed. But I miss so much I can never again have." His earlier fury subsided; he now appeared reflective. "And I'm not going to spend my life yearning for the past and hating the present." He stopped talking and held his body taut, appearing to sense something I couldn't.

"And with that, I'm off. Take care, dude." He flashed a maniacal look at me as he brushed by and took off down the stairs. I just stood there for a moment, watching him rapidly descend away from me. Then a brief rumbling sound made its way up to me. It grew louder, and I felt a brief shaking below my feet. It was the subway, making its last run of the night. Pete disappeared from view right as understanding stabbed into me.

The instant I had an inkling I moved faster than I ever have in my life. I took the stairs six at a time, holding the railings in case I took a misstep. Tears were in my eyes when my feet finally planted on the platform floor, anguish vying with terror for possession of my body.

I looked up and saw Mack and Finn standing on our side of the sparsely populated platform. Apparently they had decided to wait up for us—probably a good idea, since Finn was currently bent over a trash can repeating Mack's earlier performance. Mack stopped patting Finn on the back when he saw Pete racing along the yellow line bordering the tracks.

"Hey, buddy! Just in time for the last train!" he yelled, his voice booming down the tracks. They were a couple of hundred feet away from me. Pete was about halfway in-between, and the rumbling of the train grew louder each second. Peering ahead past our friends, I saw the dark tunnel light up with the train's headlight. So did Pete, and he stopped where he was.

Finn, having heard Mack yell out, pulled his head out of the garbage and looked towards Pete as well. Neither of them understood yet. I continued to run as fast as I could to where he stood.

"Pete, NO!" I roared before taking a quick breath. "Guys, stop him!"

A combination of my words and seeing the train emerge from the tunnel quickly allowed them to reach the same conclusion. As drunk as they both were, the same fear that propelled me immediately jolted them into action and they began sprinting as well. Too little too late. I, however, was only about thirty feet away and still had a chance to save him from the train barreling down the tracks.

Every time the subway arrived I was impressed with its sheer force, magnified by the tunnel it operated in. I would do my best not to flinch as I stood near the yellow line and faced the oncoming train, but even when I managed not to blink I failed to prevent my heart from jumping into my throat.

Pete glanced down at the tracks and the oncoming train, gauging them both. Making his choice, he straightened his shoulders and glanced back at me. We made eye contact, but even as I willed him silently to stop I knew he was beyond my persuasion. I was just a few strides away and preparing to launch myself when a devastating fact became clear. I was helpless. I wouldn't be able to stop him from jumping. And neither could anyone else.

One second stretched itself into eternity. In that second Pete turned his tear-streaked face away from mine and threw himself off of the platform. His slender body extended into the air and held itself there. Pete Hollis.

The next second struck like a lightning bolt. His body descended from its leap and onto the tracks right as the squealing train roared by. I heard a sickening smack and the squeal of the brakes. By the next second I was already fetal, collapsed on the platform. I heard screams, but I was already beyond them, my body violently shaking on the cold concrete. As subsequent seconds rolled by I didn't breathe, a fact I only realized once my body finally let out a gasping breath so it could inhale another. Then I vomited. Once, twice, and a third time.

Some time later, after the sirens had faded, I felt a hand close over my shoulder. I recognized it as Mack's and slowly lifted my face from the sidewalk bench. He was kneeling next to me, grief still pouring out of his eyes.

"He was so cold, Muff. When they took him away. He felt so cold. How could he already be so cold?"

I looked at him and felt something evaporate within. Then I felt nothing.

15

THE VALEDICTORIANS

ICE STILL FLOWED through my veins when Mack, Finn, and I finally came home that night. I walked through the door, down the hall, and into Pete's room. My roommates held back at the doorway, watching me. It smelled in here, a natural result of Pete's recent days of closed-door seclusion. I'm sure he never even noticed, as focused as he was on the book.

Glancing around, with Pete's death fresh in my mind, I mentally painted a different picture of my friend. The huge "Fulton" banner on his wall. His diploma prominently displayed. Tons of pictures spread out everywhere. Pictures of his friends and Nora. Weird that I hadn't realized how many pictures of him and Nora he still had, including a framed one near his bed. Naturally, there were no pictures of his family.

There was his gigantic desk. Made of mahogany and apparently used by his grandfather, it weighed an unbelievable amount, as we found out trying to move it in. Perched on this magnificent desk was a beat up old laptop, the same one his parents had bought him before he came to Fulton as a freshman. Resting on top of that was a binder, similar to that in which we stored our senior theses. Feeling Mack and Finn's eyes on me, I made my way over and gently picked it up. It *was* his senior thesis binder, but he had taped a piece of paper over the original cover. On the new cover was a printed picture of Fulton's quad with "The Valedictorians" scribbled in cursive above it.

I held it for a few seconds, refusing to open it. Pete's death had cast a whole new light on his writings. No longer were they the inspired words of a man reborn. I debated for a moment whether or not to open it. I had already lost so much when he jumped; did I want to dismantle my memory of him even further by exposing myself to the unhinged ramblings of a disturbed friend? I was sure he thought his writing was special and profound while he toiled away in a vacuum, but I was not convinced others, including myself, would see it in the same light.

Or it could be a balm, soothing the open wound his passing had created. I jerked open the binder and gazed inside, ignoring the small piece of paper which slipped out and fluttered to the floor. It had a cover page, and on that cover page was written:

The Valedictorians
By Pete Hollis

Dedicated to Nora, Muff, and all the other valedictorians at Fulton

I flipped the page. There was no chapter title, but in the top right hand corner "freshman year" was written in italics. Above the first paragraph, in small bold letters, was a date. September 5th, 2000. That day, I could only assume, was Pete's first at Fulton. Below it he began:

> I'm walking around campus. My parents left a half hour ago after helping me unpack. My room is still a mess, but my roommate isn't supposed to be here until tomorrow so I left it as is. It can wait. I take a seat next to an old oak in the middle of the quad of my new home and glance around. Incoming first-years walk about on this sun-dappled day with their parents in tow, trying to cover their eagerness and fear under a veil of cool. It's funny, but I see a similar attitude from the upperclassmen. They hide it better, but they're excited as well, talking animatedly as they walk with purpose amongst small groups of their peers. The energy

is infectious, and even though I am trying to take a step back from all the madness I can't help but feel like my nerve endings are on fire. All these kids, all these eclectic souls, crammed onto this little campus for the next four years of their lives. The possibilities seem endless. Not to disparage my life thus far, but I am more engaged with my surroundings this instant than at any moment in all my eighteen years previous.

As I survey the bustling campus I can't help feel like a painter staring at a blank canvas while hundreds of paints surround him, vibrant colors waiting to be utilized. I promise myself right then I will not leave Fulton with a single regret. This is a privilege, an opportunity to grow unfettered. The only thing preventing my success here is my own hesitance. And there will be none of that. I look across the quad to the entrance to the campus café, where another group of freshmen is emerging from lunches with their parents. As the parents chat with the other parents, the kids introduce themselves to each other, nervous but open.

One in particular, a blonde girl, stands out. She is flowing rather than walking, with a smile that is impossible for the other freshmen, guys or girls, to not return. Not classically gorgeous, but that doesn't stop me from immediately wanting her more than any other girl I have ever seen. She is also holding another guy's hand. Must be a high school boyfriend. A relationship that's already guaranteed to fail. I'm done romanticizing, so I pick myself up and head down to introduce myself. I will soon find out her name is Nora Williamson.

That ended the first of what I realized was a series of diary entries. The next took place that same night and described a huge party in Kerry House that I remembered attending. His attention to detail was astounding as he recounted the minutiae of that night, listing off notable people and impressions he had from his first big college party. I always knew Pete had a remarkable memory, but as I skimmed from page to page I came to the conclusion that I had drastically underestimated its extent. This wasn't a piece of historical fiction; it was a series of primary documents siphoned directly from his mind onto the paper. Despite often reflecting on college and the memories I had from it, it was only upon seeing Pete's meticulous recitation that I was struck by how much I had forgotten. All of this was true, an exhaustive recounting of the entirety of the collegiate experience as seen through the eyes of one who had taken part in all of it. Pete participating in a classroom debate with his professor, Pete attending a kegger, Pete losing his virginity to Nora, Pete hanging out in his dorm with his friends, and even Pete occasionally attending chapel, something I was unaware that he ever did. There was little to nothing of the outside world included here, just occasional mentions of his family. The world he was describing at Fulton was blissfully immersed in itself, oblivious to external stimuli.

I skimmed through, knowing I would read it over in-depth the next day. After the first seventy-five pages the header on the pages changed to "sophomore year," and then after seventy-five more it changed to "junior year," in which he included the semester he spent abroad in Germany. The narrative (despite it being a series of diary entries Pete made sure to have a cohesive flow throughout) finally transitioned over to senior year, culminating around page 300 with his final speech on graduation night, written exactly as I remember it being spoken. Then, a few lines below the conclusion of the speech, was this sentence:

A life lived for the moment is a life lived for eternity

I lifted my head from Pete's writing and glanced to the door. Both Mack and Finn had left the doorway, but were still visible as they sat slumped over on the kitchen table. Mack was snoring softly. Closing the book and then the door to the room, I softly made my way over to where my roommates dozed. I placed the binder between their two sleeping faces, turned off the light in the kitchen, and began to make my way to my own bed. Then I remembered. The piece of paper. I walked back into Pete's room and, after a quick search, discovered the scrap of notebook which had been tucked into the book. On it, scribbled almost unintelligibly, was:

> *Muff, I'm so sorry. I just don't feel it anymore, and I don't see how I will ever again. You'll be fine. You always were better than I was. Tell Nora that I never stopped loving her.*
> *-your friend forever, Pete*

Now the tears came unbidden to my eyes. I stood there and stared at that piece of paper while they trickled down my cheeks. Leaning against the wall for support, I silently cried until there was nothing left to shed. Then I folded up the piece of paper, walked into my room, and tucked it into the frame of a picture of Pete, Nora, Kate, and me that was on my bureau. It would stay there, never to be read again.

I was exhausted, but I didn't immediately join the slumber which Mack and Finn were partaking in. I lay on my bed, in the dark, and I stared at the ceiling. Pete had left behind something precious before he left, there was no doubting that. His book would help to sustain memories of him and the years we spent together, to continuously provide a reminder of a promising life lost too soon.

But I had lost so much more than that when he jumped. Reading that book dozens of times wouldn't help to fill the hollow space I acutely felt inside of me. In spite of his life's stumbles since college, I had still been projecting onto him the hopes I held for myself. It had been a rough transition from Fulton, but he had turned the corner and so had I. Except he hadn't. He had chosen to write about the good old days and then kill himself. He had failed in the worst way. I knew then I wasn't going to take the job downtown. The confidence, the ebullient attitude I had possessed just twelve hours ago, was gone. Replacing it was one image.

There he was. Hanging in the air above the tracks. I couldn't get the outline of his doomed body out of my head for weeks. But that moment, there lying in my bed, it briefly faded. In its place was the memory of graduation day and the look on his face when he entered our room to tell me about Nora. That stare had contained equal parts fear and self-hatred. It was like he had no idea how he had ended up in that predicament, and all his desperate, grasping mind could muster was revulsion at itself.

It was the same look he had given me right before he jumped.

*****

It was only natural that Pete's friends, mourning the sudden and devastating loss, would desire to read his final words. In fact, immediately after the funeral Tom, Liz, and Ben all approached me. We all had not seen each other since that night a few days previous, and when I looked into their eyes I saw the same hollowness I felt. After hugging me Tom spoke.

"Hey Muff, you have a hard copy of the book, right?"

"Yeah, it's sitting on his bed right now." For an instant I felt really possessive; up until that point only Finn, Mack, and I had read it. It was like our sacred tome, belonging only to the apartment and Pete's remaining roommates.

"Did you read it?"

"Yeah, I did. It's an amazing read, more or less a history of Pete's time at Fulton. Everything important he experienced, and his attention to detail is unbelievable. All three of you are in there." They all brightened at that last sentence, excited at the prospect of having their memories of Pete related back to them by Pete himself.

"So, would it be cool if we borrowed it?" Liz tentatively asked.

"I could just email you a copy." I immediately knew something wasn't quite right about that suggestion. Liz's reaction confirmed it.

"Yeah, I suppose. But, I don't know, I think we would all prefer to have the copy he made for you guys." Tom and Ben nodded their heads in agreement.

I understood. The words themselves were powerful, but there was something about reading Pete's personal copy that added even more intimacy to the experience.

"Okay, I don't see a problem with that. You guys will love it."

Tom smiled. "I'm sure we will. I want to see what shit he made up about me."

That night when Finn, Mack, and I went back the apartment, Tom came with us. We all stood in Pete's room staring at *The Valedictorians* as it lay on his bed. Mack and Finn had both read it the next day, and had been brought to tears as well. Tom stepped forward and gently picked it up.

"Guys, I promise I'll take care of it. And I'll have it back in a week once Ben, Liz, and I have all had a chance to read it. Mint condition."

I stared at the book while he said this, still unwilling to let it leave our custody, but eventually it did. I wasn't that anxious though; I knew they would take great care of it.

A week later it came back in much the same condition. Ben returned the book, looking mildly awed as he told me I should have read a passage from it for Pete's eulogy. I would have, but Pete's dad had given the eulogy, somberly recounting memories he had of Pete growing up. I hadn't heard any of these stories. For all I knew, Pete was born the instant he set foot on Fulton's campus.

A couple of days later our friends Johann and Kyle, who were roommates, showed up. They said how they had also wondered about the book, and heard from Liz that we had let her borrow it. Could they borrow it too? I couldn't refuse, and, once again, the book was taken only to be returned in a week's time with profuse thanks. Thus a pattern was started. Word spread quickly, in the Boston area and soon beyond it. Every week an old friend of Pete's would show up at our apartment asking to borrow the original version of *The Valedictorians*. If we told them someone else currently was reading it, they just asked us to let them know when we had it again. Some friends in distant locales were emailed copies, but many made trips to Boston just to read the official bound copy. A waiting list formed, getting as long as a dozen people before the end of the summer finally brought about a decline in requests. By then well over a hundred people had read Pete's autobiography, and not a single one didn't let us know how glad they were that they did. I always knew Pete was popular, but only then did the true extent of his reach become apparent.

*****

That October, as another fall was beginning to reveal itself in the changing leaves, another visitor showed up at the apartment wanting to read *The Valedictorians*. We had signed up for another year in the same place, deciding that the lingering positive memories of Pete outweighed the horrific finale of his life. Rather than get another person to move into the room, we preferred to each pay an extra 175 dollars a month in rent.

Mack and Finn had both left for the weekend, so it was me that answered the knock that afternoon. I opened the door and there she was, wearing a green sundress on an unseasonably warm day. She looked up at me and let a beautiful, melancholy smile spread across her face. I had heard Nora was stateside since graduating from Oxford, but I was still completely caught off-guard.

"Hi, Sam. It's been awhile." Tears were visible in her eyes. I didn't know what to say, so I just walked up and gave her a big hug. I could feel the moisture from her face on my neck as she embraced me and quietly sobbed. We held each other for a minute before I led her inside the house.

I had forgotten what a profound and immediate impression she made. Seeing her again, I was almost tempted to think that dating her had been Pete's greatest accomplishment, because she was the most impressive girl I had ever known. Even now, distraught, she still maintained the grace that came so naturally to her. Her previously long blond hair was now short, which only served to draw more attention to her sparkling blue eyes. It also made her look older and I had to confess that, in the two years since I had last seen, her she had left behind all but a few vestiges of the girl I knew at Fulton.

I kept the copy of *The Valedictorians* on the nightstand next to my bed, but now it lay on our coffee table between Nora and me. She had stopped crying, which I was thankful for. To see a girl like her cry was like watching someone piss on a Monet. It just wasn't right. Her gaze alternating between the book and me, she started talking.

"I'm so sorry I couldn't make it to the funeral. It tore me up inside, but I just didn't have enough money to fly out from Oxford. You understand, right?"

I nodded my head in understanding, feeling bad that she still felt guilty. It wasn't as if Pete wouldn't have understood.

"Anyways, I finished up my art history degree there in the spring, and I'm working at an auction house in New York. I'm living there with a guy I met in Oxford. His name is Peter too. Weird, right? The thing is, my entire time at Oxford I always held out hope that Pete would at least call. I missed him so much, but I just couldn't forgive him for what he did right away. Plus, deep down, I believed that I would see him again, and when I did I would know for sure if we were meant to be with each other." Her voice caught there, but after a couple of seconds she regained her composure and looked up at me.

"And now this," she said as she gestured to the book. "This is all that's left." She leaned over, gently lifting it. "I heard he was writing a book a couple of weeks before he died. I was so happy. I always told him he would be a great writer."

Pausing, she stared at what Pete had done. "I didn't hear he actually finished it until a couple months ago. Tom was down visiting New York and he told me he had read it and how great it was. He said the amount of detail was astonishing. Pete had such a great memory. He could always remember the tiniest details about moments we shared. Every little anniversary, every special time." She let the book rest in her lap, placing her hands on it as she regarded me with haunted eyes.

"You've read it, right Sam?"

"Yeah, lots of times. I can hear him speaking every word in it, and when I read it I kind of forget he's gone."

Nora appeared to consider my words and then come to a decision. She stood up with the book clutched in her palms.

"Do you mind if I go into his room and read it?

"Right now? Well, there isn't any furniture in there. But I can bring you a chair."

She waved me off. "No, I don't need a chair. I'll just sit on his floor." I led her to his room and watched as she cracked a wry smile at the "Pete's Palace" strip club poster that his parents had understandably let us keep.

"I remember when he got that poster junior year. He thought it was so great. Glad you guys kept it up."

I laughed. "Yeah, I couldn't bring myself to take it down. I think the room really became his when he nailed that thing up there. And it's still his as long as it stays up."

Nora gave me a look that made it clear she wanted to be alone with the book, so I smiled and told her if she needed anything to let me know. Closing the door, I left her with her and Pete's memories.

I lost track of the time, and it was night when she emerged, book cradled under her arm. I was on the couch watching the TV, which I immediately flipped off when she came into view. It was clear she had been crying more, but also obvious was the air of serenity that surrounded her. Like everyone else who had read Pete's history, it had apparently done much to heal the pain left by his passing.

She gingerly placed the book on the couch next to me, letting her fingers slowly slide off its cover.

"So, feeling any better?" I said as I rose off the couch.

"Much." She leaned over and kissed me on the cheek. "Thank you for that. Tell Mack and Finn I'm sorry I missed them, and that I will be really angry if they don't visit next time they're in New York. The same goes for you. And I promise the next time I'm here we'll go out and have a great time. Maybe I'll bring Peter. He's really a great guy, and I think you'd like him a lot." She walked over to where she had placed her bag, tossed it over her shoulder, and came back to hug me goodbye.

"He left a note, Nora. A goodbye note in the book. To both you and me."

She stopped a foot away from me, and a bit of the previous haunted look returned. "What did it say?"

"It said he was sorry, and it told me to tell you that he never stopped loving you."

She flinched, but her eyes never left my own. She looked much older than her twenty-four years right then, and I felt much older than mine.

"Well, that's good to hear, Sam. I never stopped loving him, not even now. It's just too bad he had to stop loving life, because he was the best thing to ever happen to mine."

We hugged for what seemed like an eternity, and when we broke apart my eyes were moist.

"Take care, Sam."

"You too, Nora."

She gave one last look towards the book, then turned and walked out the door, effectively closing that chapter of her life. As I glanced at the novel and its author's empty room, I wondered if I would be able to do the same. I had my doubts.

16

DATE NIGHT

MY DATE WITH Lucie was going well. Real well. After our Thai dinner we migrated to a bar near where I lived named the Cantab. Mack loved it, once even stumbling home wasted and claiming that the PBR there was better than any other PBR he had ever had. I had told Lucie my roommate highly recommended the place but not how many times he most likely had peed on the street outside of it.

As we sat across from each other grinning, I couldn't have imagined feeling happier. We both had had a few beers, but I knew that the alcohol wasn't why I felt so comfortable in her presence. The moment she had shown up outside the restaurant all the worries that had been accumulating instantly disappeared. One smile from her and my fears and doubts were rendered foolish. I couldn't fixate on my own nerves anymore. I was too immersed in her.

She talked of her family, her friends, her career goals. I did the same, carefully leaving out the goals. She had two brothers, both older, and had majored in English at Amherst. She appeared to enjoy her job at Legacy, or at least the challenges it presented, a point of view I chose not to critique. I was too busy marveling at her. This was a fascinating girl, from her laugh to the grimace she used when talking about Donald. I would have mentally kicked myself for waiting this long to ask her out, but I could barely contain my giddiness. It must have rubbed off on her too, because she seemed just as energized as I.

"So, what do you think, you want to get out of here and chill at my apartment?" I astonished myself with my boldness. I wasn't even that drunk, but my words came out sounding assured and polished. Lucie had been drinking from her glass, and her eyebrows went up slightly. She swallowed her mouthful and smiled.

"Yeah, sure, Sam. I'm interested in seeing what this place looks like. I'm guessing…a complete disaster area."

"Don't worry, I'll be dispensing gas masks at the door." She laughed and we exited the bar. On the walk over I couldn't resist touching her. I lightly brushed my fingers against hers, and in response she took my hand into her own. We walked in silence, both smiling. Then we were there.

"So where's my mask?" she asked as I fumbled with my keys at the door. I opened the door and quickly ascertained that neither Mack nor Finn were there. I had told them to make themselves scarce, but you never knew. I turned to her.

"I actually think we're out of masks."

"So what am I going to do for oxygen?" She looked mischievous, challenging me to make a move. I accepted the challenge.

"Well I think I can give you some of mine…" I said this as I leaned in. She tilted her head back and let her eyes close. Our lips met and it was exactly what I hoped for. Perfect symmetry. Our tongues lightly danced around each other as my hands wrapped around her waist and she placed her own on my chest. It was a nice change of pace not being blackout, and I suspected Beth was not nearly as good a kisser as Lucie. She would be uninventive and bland, while Lucie was proving herself to be an artist.

We stumbled in through the doorway, stopping briefly so I could kick the door shut behind us. When I turned back around she was taking off her top, revealing smooth pale skin and a surprising curvaceous figure. But before I could help her get her bra off she hurriedly asked, "Which room is yours?" I pointed down the hall to where my door was ajar and watched as she sprinted down towards it, taking her bra off as she did. I gave one look skyward, thanked Jesus, and took off after her.

When I burst into my room a couple of seconds later she was already on my bed taking off her jeans. Whatever look was on my face must have been funny, because she laughed loudly and said, "Sam, why don't you lose the clothes? It'll make all of this a lot easier."

I obliged as quickly as I could, not feeling the slightest bit self-conscious of my naked body as I slid out of my underwear and joined her on my bed. She too was now naked, but held me at arms length.

"Condom?"

"Yeah, definitely! Hold on!" I jumped back off my bed, reached into my underwear drawer, found one, and held it up triumphantly.

She laughed again. "Great. Now I would like to thank you for helping me out with the Hart outreach today, but I can't do that if you're way over there."

She thanked me, and then some. It seemed to go on for days, our bodies exploring each others like a couple of sixteen-year-olds. Once again, I was glad I wasn't hammered, because I remembered every second of it. She was so soft, from the way her skin felt to the whispered sounds she made as we rolled around my bed. And, when it was done, her breath was soft as it caressed the skin of my chest.

*****

We lay there for what felt like hours, just breathing, but still awake and acutely aware of the other. Then, her head resting on my chest, she spoke.

"What was your friend's name?" I paused for a few seconds, deciding whether or not I wanted to go down this road. She had disarmed me though, and not just because we were post-coital. I had wanted to tell her everything about myself from the moment I met her, which explained why I had been so afraid to talk to her in the first place.

"Pete."

"How did he do it?" Her voice became quieter.

"He jumped in front of an oncoming subway train. I realized too late what he was going to do, and I think he had been planning it for months. Crazy, right? I wish I could have seen it coming, but he had seemed so well before that night."

"Yeah. Definitely nuts. I'm so sorry, Sam. I don't know what I would do if one of my best friends did that. Why do you think he planned it?"

I reached over to my nightstand and picked up *The Valedictorians*. It was much more worn now than when I had first found it, but I made sure no dust accumulated in the weeks between readings. I held it in front of us, feeling renewed pride at what my friend had accomplished.

"Because Pete spent his last couple months, day and night, writing this. I think he meant it to be an elaborate obituary. He was obsessed, but we thought in a good, literary genius sort of way. It's really an engrossing read, especially if you went to Fulton with him." Lifting her head up to get a better look at the book, Lucie then turned her face back to me, regarding me with curious eyes.

"Why do you think he did it? Was he depressed? Mentally unstable? Did he get his heart broken?"

I had asked myself that question a million times, if only because I sought alternative answers other than the one I always knew to be true. It would be so much easier just to write him off as a closeted nut job, a friend who had gone off the deep end. But then I remembered his eyes at the end, and I knew he hadn't lost his mind. Perspective, maybe, but not his mind. He knew what he was throwing away, but he thought what he had lost to be that much greater and more devastating.

"Pete lost a lot when he graduated college. He lost the love of his life and he lost a place that was home to him much more than his actual home ever was. I mean, everyone loves college, but, with Pete, I think he altered himself so that he only tuned into the collegiate experience. You should have seen him at school in his element. He was something, just an amazing person in general."

I was talking about him in an analytical manner that belied the turbulent emotions boiling under the surface. I loved college almost as much as Pete did. I was extremely dissatisfied with my life since then. He just lived life on a grander scale than I did. I quietly slipped farther into obscurity each day while he took dramatic steps to end his own disgust with himself. He was dead. I didn't feel alive. Sometimes I couldn't differentiate.

"If you don't mind me saying so, for such an amazing guy he seemed to take the easy way out." Lucie's words reflected another sentiment I had internally voiced. I placed the book back on the nightstand and looked down at her. Unable to resist, I leaned down and let my lips brush against hair. She smiled back at me and waited.

"Yeah. I won't defend his actions. I can't. But…you just had to see him to understand. After Fulton he was like…a tree that had been uprooted. He tried his luck out in California, and then here in Boston, but you could see it just wasn't the right climate for him. He loved being around us but couldn't handle the new environment he found himself in. He didn't know what else to do, where else to go. Deep down, he was just scared." Images of him suspended above the subway rails flashed behind my eyes and I resisted flinching.

"That's what I saw right before he died. Fear. Anger too, but the anger came from the fear. That the best had passed him by and he was never going to be able to reclaim it."

That was the most I had ever said regarding Pete. It all tumbled out at once, but I was relieved that at least, reflecting on it, it made sense. Lucie seemed pacified by my explanation; that or she thought such a sensitive subject wasn't worth debating. But I wasn't done.

"I should have been more proactive with him," I continued. "I saw plenty of little signs, but it was easier just to assume he knew how to handle his own life. That and…" I stopped myself. I was about to say how I found his own despair reflected in myself and how I more than sympathized with his moments of terror. I lived them, and the only reason I felt even mildly comfortable discussing this was because of Lucie. I hadn't felt this safe in forever.

"That and what?" She had been stroking my hand with her fingers, but now stopped and turned her full attention back to me. My own demons were better left alone at this juncture.

"Nothing. Have you ever been in love?" She had talked of many things that night, including mentions of past boyfriends, but I wanted to know more. As much as I could.

"Ummmm" She tilted her head up in thought, letting it drop once the thought was fully formed. "Maybe? I had a boyfriend back at Amherst who I cared a lot about, but we broke it off before we each went abroad for our junior years. It's hard to say now that it's been a few years. And I just broke up with a guy I had been seeing for the past year or so who I thought at one time I loved. Now I think otherwise. You?"

I was caught off-guard by the recent boyfriend comment. Maybe it was good fortune I only asked her out just now. I thought for a couple of seconds before I responded, even though I had given this topic a significant amount of consideration since I graduated.

"If you had asked me before I graduated I think I would have said yes. Now, a couple of years later, I don't know. I'll say yes, but it's a tentative yes."

Lucie went back to stroking my hand. "So what made you ask that question?"

"Just curious. But I also wonder if Pete could have weathered the storm if he had still been with his girlfriend from college." A car alarm went off in the distance, and Lucie waited until it finished before responding.

"Yeah, Sam, I see what you're saying, but another person can never cure your own dissatisfaction with yourself. You have to find true happiness from within, and if you're looking to fix your life by getting into relationships, you're bound to be disappointed."

"I don't know about that." I smiled down at her. "You made me pretty happy tonight."

She returned the smile. "Well, orgasms will do that to you. Unfortunately, I don't think you can achieve happiness through orgasms alone."

"No?"

"Well…" I felt her hand trace down from my belly button. "That doesn't mean their value should ever be overlooked."

I felt my blood pressure rise, among other things. "Yeah, I couldn't agree more. Certain things just can't be taken for granted."

Afterwards, for the first time in a long time, I didn't fear sleep and the tomorrow it was a bridge to. If tomorrow involved waking up next to Lucie, I was perfectly content allowing my consciousness to drift away. When I finally succumbed, no nightmare dared trouble me. For one night at least I was protected.

17

SURPRISE, SURPRISE

WAKING UP WAS never so easy. It was almost noon when my eyes opened, and the first thing they gazed upon was Lucie. One red curl hung down over her slumbering face, matching the dash of freckles across her nose and cheeks. If anything, I was more thunderstruck than last night. It wasn't that I had had sex with her. I had had sex with girls since Kate. But, when I woke up the next morning, both parties would don a mask. The post-hookup mask. Wearing this mask, each refuses to give away their true feelings about the other. Their faces are neutral and superficially polite, resulting with neither knowing where the other stands on what had happened. With me it had been easy because I had felt nothing for any of them.

My defenses weren't up, and they weren't going to go up once she awoke. I felt vulnerable, but I embraced it. It meant I cared enough to be nervous. I decided earlier that there would be no posturing if I was lucky enough to end up in this kind of situation with her. I sought for there to be no confusion between us about how I felt, and even if she was guarded I wouldn't waver. I was sold on the transformative power of Lucie Mallory and I wasn't going to let her think otherwise.

Half conscious but sensing me looking at her, Lucie fluttered her eyelids and slowly let her green eyes focus on my own. This was a big moment, at least for me. A couple of seconds passed as we regarded each other, faces a foot apart. Then she reached up and grabbed my nose.

"Honk!"

I felt my face split into a grin, which she returned. But before I could kiss her she laughed and spun out of bed.

"Hey, where are you going?" I meant my words to have some force behind them, indicating how much I wanted her to come back to bed, but they lost their power as I observed her naked form. She wasn't bothering to cover up as she walked around the room searching for her clothes. "It's only noon. We still have a whole afternoon to stay in bed."

She looked up and smiled as she pulled her newly discovered underwear up her legs. "That does sound tempting, but I have to meet a friend for lunch at one. So no time to dillydally."

I started to object but decided against it. Just because I wasn't going to hide how I felt didn't mean I was going to act like a needy little bitch. People had different ways of expressing themselves, and maybe Lucie was just as giddy as I was. Pulling myself upright, I spotted her bra underneath my nightstand.

"Yo. Catch." I made sure to get one last good look as she spun around, then I tossed it over. Once the bra was on I quietly sighed and began looking for my boxers. When I finally discovered them Lucie was fully dressed. I quickly jerked them up under the covers and rolled out of the bed to stand in front of her. Since she was the one in the hurry, I decided to let her set the tone for the farewell.

"Well, that was a lot of fun. I'm really glad we did it." She was smiling, but I didn't sense the infatuation I possessed. Affection, but from a distance. That distance shrunk as she took a couple of steps and put her hands on my shoulders. I got shivers just from feeling her skin, and the pleasure multiplied exponentially when she leaned in and let her lips press against mine. I kissed back and both our mouths opened. Lying dormant since we had awoken, the passion quickly reignited as our tongues moved together, shyly getting reacquainted. But, right as my hands slipped to her waist and started to draw her close, she pulled away. My only solace was that it was with reluctance that she did so. But why? Why was she fighting it?

She wasn't smiling as she looked at me from a safe distance. She looked…worried? I couldn't tell.

"Okay. Like I said, I had a great time. But I really got to get going."
She waited a couple of seconds, and, not seeing an immediate response,
began to move towards the door.

"So is it cool if I call? You know, to try to arrange another great
time?" I sounded more confident than I felt, but I sensed that this wasn't
the time to sound unsure of myself.

Lucie gave me another indecipherable look. After a couple of seconds
she realized she had to say something and settled on the words. "Yeah, sure,
give me a ring." If it had been any other girl I would have been skeptical.
But the connection we shared was undeniable and could overcome whatever
reservations she had. Right? I thought that I at least had a fragile faith in that.

"Cool. Enjoy the lunch. And...you're beautiful." That was apparently
all I could come up with for a romantic line. Maybe it was the unbelievably
awkward delivery, but she couldn't suppress her amusement.

"Thanks, Sam. Enjoy your Saturday. And put some pants on." She
turned and walked out of the room. I waved at her back, and when that
disappeared I listened to her open and close the front door. Then she was
gone. I stood there in my underwear, mulling how enthused I should be.
I decided not very, but that I would still give her a call tomorrow. She was
an oasis in my desert, and I had no choice but to drink deeply.

*****

"What is it? What's changed? When did you become a player? Two
hotties in three nights? What the fuck, dude?" Mack stared across the
kitchen table, awed by what he saw in front of him. I tried my best to ignore
my friend, preferring to act fascinated by the cereal I was spooning into my
mouth. After our uncomfortable goodbye the last thing I wanted to think
about was Lucie. I silently cursed how fleeting happiness could be.

"What was this one's name?" He was determined to get some
answers, so I indulged his curiosity.

"Lucie. Another girl from work."

"Another one? Dude, you're breaking the 'don't shit where you eat'
rule. Don't make me go to your office and put up fliers with your mug
shot on it to warn the women of a predator in their midst."

I laughed. "You think Lucie's pretty hot though?"

"More your type than mine. But yeah, she's still out of your league."

"Thanks, buddy."

"No problem. You seem pretty into her though. She going to take my place in the house when I leave? Maybe she could bring a friend to live in Pete's room, save you some rent?"

"What are you talking about? You're leaving?" Resting my spoon on my bowl's edge, I regarded Mack with something nearing hostility. Where was this coming from? I had heard nothing of him leaving.

Now he was the one on the defensive. He looked at me in brief confusion, which quickly shifted to awkward embarrassment. "Yeah, I guess I didn't tell you yet. I just realized that. I told Finn last night when we both were out downtown."

"You're leaving? Where for?" the acid in my eyes now sunk into my voice, and Mack blanched visibly. He really didn't have anything to be ashamed of, but he was a big softie at heart and I knew that. What I was doing was really indefensible, but I didn't give a shit anymore.

"My dad got me a job at his bank in Philadelphia. He said it was about time I did something worthwhile with my life and that this would be his one offer to help me out. So I took it. I'm starting the beginning of June, and I'll leave the apartment in a few weeks." Not seeing my annoyance diminish, he continued. "Don't worry, Muff, I'll get someone else to sublet, and if I don't I'll pay for the apartment until I do. And I was only kidding about your girl staying here."

"She's not my girl. You're leaving in a few weeks? For Philadelphia? What the fuck?"

"Yeah, it's kind of sudden, right? Well, I figured I just turned twenty-five and I better get myself a real job. Time to stop dicking around, you know?"

I hated him then. Hated his privileged existence. Hated how he, with one call to daddy, had pulled himself out of the hole he had previously shared with me. I waited a long while before responding, fiddling around with my cereal while he looked at me anxiously. Once the bile had diminished I looked up at him.

"Hey, congrats, dude. That's really nice of your dad. It's going to be weird not having you around. We had quite the run together."

He looked relieved. "Yeah, about seven years, right? But don't worry, Muff, it's not like we can't visit. Philly isn't far away. And nothing's stopping you from moving down there. Shake things up. We've been in Boston long enough."

"I could move down to Philly. Nothing's stopping me." I said this more to myself than to the man facing me across the table. But why the fuck would I move down to Philly? There was as much waiting for me there as there was keeping me here. Jack shit. I had trouble gathering the motivation to get out of bed, let alone pack up and move. I shook my head.

"Muff? You alright?"

"Yeah, I'm fine. Just thinking. Maybe. Who knows? Well, let's at least make sure your last weeks in Boston aren't sober. You're down to go out tonight, right?" This was a rhetorical question.

"Um, I actually don't think I can, dude," Mack replied guiltily. "I kind of have a date tonight. Friend of the family who's in town. My parents told her to look me up. I haven't seen her in a few years, but I remember her being a babe. How about tomorrow?"

I got some measure of solace from the fact that he was willing to get hammered on a Sunday night, but it wasn't enough.

"Yeah, we'll see, man."

Mack looked ready to say something else when Finn poked his head into the kitchen. Something was up with him. I had hadn't seen him this cheerful in months. Unabashed joy lit up his face. Medical school. That had to be it. My happiness for my friend was tempered by a mild sinking sensation in my chest. Of the six schools he had applied for, only one, Harvard, was in the Boston area.

"Ahem." Finn pulled his hand from behind the doorframe, and in it was one piece of paper. The name of the school was legible from where Mack and I sat. Duke. It had been Finn's number one choice. "Check it out, gentlemen. I'm in. Med school, here I come."

"Congrats, man!" Mack was already on his feet and walking over. I quickly followed suit, my elation for Finn outweighing my initial self-pity. We both embraced him at once, Mack taking the liberty of mussing up his hair. We broke apart, all three of us with a hand on another's shoulders as we savored Finn's success.

"So when are you leaving Boston?" I made myself ask the question. Finn's expression turned slightly melancholy as he scrutinized me.

"Not too long after Mack leaves, I suspect. Probably the middle of May. They have a summer program down there I enrolled in. I'll get someone to sublet, and if I can't I have enough money to pay off the rest of the rent. But we should get you some company for this big old apartment. I bet there is some Fulton kid who needs a place. Or maybe someone at my lab. I'll ask around."

Silence settled in when I didn't respond. I didn't know what the say. My two best friends were leaving me in the next month. I felt a stabbing pang of sorrow but shook it off, acutely aware of my roommates' examining eyes.

Finn gave my shoulder a squeeze and let go. "Okay, Mack, you ready? It starts at two." I had forgotten. The memorial service in Natick was this afternoon.

"Yep. All set."

"You're not going to dress up any more than that?" Finn said as he gave a skeptical look at Mack's hoodie and jeans. "Maybe a nice collared shirt?"

"Whatever. This is nice enough. Pete wouldn't have cared."

"You sure you don't want to come, dude?" Finn said this to me without any recrimination in his voice. He knew, as all of our friends knew, how much Pete's passing had affected me. I had nothing else to say on the matter, especially not some clichéd words over his grave.

I shook my head. "No dude, I think I'll stick around here. Maybe go on a run or something."

Mack and Finn both nodded their heads understandingly.

"I'll tell Pete's parents you give your best." Finn said. "And I plan on going out tonight to celebrate the med school acceptance if you're down. I could use a wingman since hotstuff over here has a date." He looked back at Mack in mild disapproval. "Let's go, Versace."

They walked out the door, leaving me alone at a kitchen table in a silent house. This would be a situation I would have to get used to.

18

MEMORIAL

I FOUGHT IT, but before long my thoughts were drifting back to Pete. Lucie could be credited with keeping my mind off him in the last day, but with her status now uncertain there was one concrete fact I couldn't escape. Pete had been gone a year and there was nothing I could do to bring him back. He had left me to fend for myself, to make my way in a world that I felt more and more removed from every day.

I had been sitting at the table for some time, just staring off into space and letting vague memories of my dead friend flit in and out of my brain. Worrying I would get lost in one, I didn't focus on any particular recollection for more than a couple of seconds. It was a legitimate fear. If you let it, the past will unravel you. Fiber by fiber, you will come undone until nothing solid is left. The temptation is to walk backwards towards your own death, staring only at the beautiful wasteland of the life you have left behind. I could think of nothing more appealing right now.

Eventually I became too agitated. The solution was clear. I walked over to the fridge and pulled open the door, finding a fair amount of beer inside. I was pretty sure I had bought it, but couldn't remember when. Grabbing a couple, I immediately went to work. Sure, it was only two p.m., but it was a Saturday, which provided me with the illusion I was getting an early start on an epic night. Six empty bottles and sixty minutes later I was feeling much better. I was numb, but that was exactly what I wanted. This allowed me to believe myself powerful and dangerous. Not bothering to grab my coat, I made my way out the door and into the crisp spring afternoon.

I began to walk, seemingly without purpose, grinning at any girls I passed with the confidence of a drunk who believes himself above suspicion. Making my way down the street, I was only vaguely aware of the life around me; my mind was more concerned with each step I took. I watched one foot follow the other, curious as to where I was leading myself. I still hadn't decided, but I had an idea of where I might end up. That suspicion was confirmed when I let my legs come to an abrupt stop in front of the doors with a "Red Line" sign above them.

I must have ridden on the subway at least a couple dozen times in the past year, but each was just as distressing as the last. I was thankful I had the luxury of being able to drive to work, because there was no way I could cope with riding the T every morning. However, today I had an explicit purpose propelling me forward. I wasn't taking the subway to head to some bar or a friend's house; I was riding the underground train right into the heart of my trauma. I was bound for the Truman T stop where Pete had ended his life.

I wished I had managed to down a couple of more bottles before I left, conveniently forgetting that in my haste to get drunk I had vomited in the back of my throat a few times. What alcohol I currently had running in my blood did provide a necessary cushion, making me only half aware when the train finally screamed into the station. It seemed slower, less ferocious then when it had slammed into Pete's crouched body on the tracks. I still cringed visibly when it went by, staring straight at the floor and holding my breath until it finally came to a stop. The doors finally opened and I made sure I was the first one safely inside, knowing that once I was nestled in a seat I could stare at the advertisements and other passengers without having to acknowledge I could have been riding in the same train that had taken Pete from this earth. That was something I couldn't afford to consider.

Back in September of 2005, in the time before Legacy when I had been temping, I was forced to ride the T every day to get downtown. I say "forced," but eight-year old Sam wouldn't have considered it a burden at all. In first grade, my science class had taken a field trip to the Boston

Museum of Science. This journey, I was ecstatic to find out, would involve my classmates and I traveling on the subway. I still remember now how wound up I was when we descended down the escalators into the high-tech underground city full of roaring trains and booming intercoms. Overwhelmed by just the station, I could hardly control my senses when my fellow first graders and I boarded the train and shot into the darkness ahead, our vice-like little hands gripping the bars a little tighter as we prepared to never return to the surface. I recall at one point thinking I could get used to the life of a mole, but then they we were, speeding out into the daylight and over a bridge, the skyline of Boston in front of our eyes.

It took me about ten seconds into my first day of temping for that elation to wear off. I was just a guy in business casual among many other guys in business casual, all of whom could care less that they were riding modern public transportation. It was just another way to get around. However, riding the subway did grant an intimate proximity to a diverse group of people, and I have always had a powerful interest in the observation of my fellow humans. I took a brief hiatus from thinking about Pete and tried to observe my fellow riders this Saturday afternoon.

No businessmen were riding, but businessmen were the least remarkable. Directly across from me was an Asian couple, sitting in silence. The only evidence they were together was that the woman would occasionally look at her partner's stoic face as if seeking some answer to a question she had yet to ask. After a half minute both lifted their eyes to stare at me and I was forced to direct my gaze to a girl a couple of seats over. I was pleased to notice that, not only was she cute, but she had been staring at me before I met her glance. I never knew how to take that. I often stared at people just because I desired something to stare at, but as a guy my first impulse when I made eye contact with an attractive girl was to consider her a sexual target. A typical drunk reaction would be to make it clear I liked looking at her as well and advance a dopey smile in her direction, but this afternoon was not a typical afternoon and I wasn't going to waste any energy on her. Finally, I let my eyes drift to my left and the guy standing there. He looked horrible. About my age by the looks of it, slightly slouched, his gaze was fixed on the other set of doors. There was nothing there to look at, but still he stared with a disturbing intensity. Lips downturned, deep dark circles under his eyes, and possessing at least a few days stubble, he glared, oblivious to the world around him. I suspected I could stare forever without him noticing but, even with that understanding, observing him made me self-conscious. It made me question what I looked like to the others around me. I looked away and trained my eyes on the floor in front of my feet, doing my best to keep my mind blank until we got the Truman Station.

I was so successful at spacing out that I almost missed the stop, barely squeezing through the closing doors as they shut. And then there I was, back at Truman Station for the first time since Pete had left me. During my previous subway trips in the past year I had made a conscious point to never get off or open my eyes at Truman, but now I stood at the largely empty subway platform unsure what to think. It was the afternoon, not the night like before, but you couldn't tell the difference down here. Pete might be buried in some field in Natick where Mack and Finn were paying their respects, but as far as I was concerned this is where he would always be entombed. Underneath a city that had helped to destroy him.

I wandered, still drunk, to the set of tracks where he had jumped. When I got to the edge of the platform I clumsily sat down and let my legs dangle over. Gently letting them swing back and forth, I stared at roughly the same spot where he had taken his last breath. This was where Pete had died a year ago. I tried to comprehend what it meant to me that instant, but all I could feel in my head was the fog from the alcohol. I was content with leaving my emotions distant and almost considered leaving, but then the distant noises of the oncoming train drifted down the tunnel. With that faraway screech I time-traveled.

There I was, screaming. There was Pete, jumping. There were Mack and Finn, eyes wide and unbelieving. The memory ripped at my soul and threatened to tear it asunder. What could he have been thinking, that last split second? Did his life flash before his eyes? Did he feel a weight being lifted, a sensation of calm? Or, was it what I feared the most: that in that last moment he regretted his decision and wished he could have escaped his fate? That possibility made me nauseous, that when it was clear he had lost everything he had wanted nothing more than to have it all back. I would never know; I could never ask him.

A horn sounded. The train was closer now, and as I glanced down the tracks into the black tunnel beyond I could begin to make out its lights. No one had told me to get away from the edge yet. I found that interesting. Did they just not care, or were they secretly hoping I would follow in Pete's footsteps? They might get their wish, because I was giving it some serious consideration. A slideshow of Pete's life at Fulton and beyond played in my head, only the last slide remaining incomplete. Was his death a blessing or a curse?

The train was almost in sight now, but before it could get any closer I felt a hand come to rest on my shoulder. It was a T worker, looking at me with a mixture of concern and suspicion. I raised myself to my feet and apologized, saying I didn't know why I was doing that. He kept on looking at me and I started smiling, stepped further and further from the tracks with my hands raised. See, nothing to worry about here. Apparently he decided I was just a space case or an attention-seeker, because he shook his head in resignation and walked away, muttering about the world going to hell. I couldn't agree more.

I wasn't going to die the way Pete died, that I knew. Being here made me ache inside, but something about this location was sacred. It was here that the finale to a great life took place, and in a perverted way Pete had claimed the spot as his own, haunting it with his spirit. I couldn't think of anyone other than him while I occupied this space, least of all myself. If I wanted to put my own life in perspective I would have to leave.

I took one last look at the tracks, soaked it in, and walked away. Nothing left to see here.

19

FACING THE END

AN HOUR LATER I was back in the house and on my way to being sober. That didn't last long. Before I was drinking for Pete; now I was drinking for me. I had a bottle of Belvedere on my desk, a bottle which began emptying itself immediately after I entered my room and closed the door. There were few better ways to spend a Saturday afternoon, especially one as nice as this. The warm spring breeze floated through the opened windows of my room, sweeping away all the musty residue of winter.

It brought with it memories of countless springs before. I was in elementary school playing kickball during recess. I was in high school, laughing with friends on the front lawn as I signed someone's yearbook. I was in college, resting my head on Kate's supple stomach on the beach at Point Pond, both of us half-heartedly trying to peruse a couple of pages of the required reading before class.

I was on my bed in my room. With a half-empty bottle of vodka on one side and a still-full bottle of sleeping pills on the other. It really was too easy to get prescription meds. Pete had had his reasons for despair, and I had mine, undermining my desire for life. I blamed the breeze.

I had realized a few months ago, when these attacks of hopelessness began to occur in increasing intervals, how fragile my existence had become. I now lived my life on a balance beam, all too aware of how close I was to falling off. I wouldn't be caught off guard by my demise;

I could see the signs a mile away and understood that, no matter how happy I might be at any given moment, all it took was a slight push and I would fall to the mat.

I tried to summon thoughts of Lucie and the events of last night, but they were scuttled by the more recent happenings of today. Maybe it was the alcohol, but I had convinced myself that the "connection" I had felt last night was imagined. Sex played tricks on one's mind. Whatever flimsy affection I might hold for her was effectively dismantled by the cold hard realism my brain had unleashed. It didn't matter what I wanted to have, all that mattered was what I currently had. Now that both Mack and Finn were leaving, what I had was nothing.

I picked up the bottle of pills, took off the cap, and proceeded to stare in at the many little harbingers of my death. Each of them would play a little part in shutting me down, leaving their own little chemical signature on my body. I wondered how many I should take. I didn't like swallowing pills; I always winced when I gulped down my multivitamin every morning. That decision could wait a little longer. I had time. Well, maybe not that much time. As more and more of the alcohol absorbed itself into my system, I found my willpower becoming hazy, my persona something detached. I was starting to think of myself from outside of myself. I was a copied version of Sam, blessed with the ability to critique but unable to initiate any action.

I remember sophomore year, when Pete, Mack, and Tom all took mushrooms. Finn and I agreed to be the designated watchers in case they did something insanely dumb. Things started off normal, but by the end of the night Pete was having a fascinating conversation with a lamp and Tom refused to leave a shower stall. Both were hilarious in their own way. Mack, however, went in a completely different direction. He had been staring at a rug for a while, so it surprised me greatly when he finally lifted up his face and made eye contact with me. I had never seen him look so intense. He gestured for me to go out into the stairwell with him and I obliged my psychedelic friend. When we got out there he spoke like a different person, quickly dissolving my patronizing attitude.

"Muff, I realized something just now. There isn't just me. There are hundreds, thousands, millions of me. I'm only living one of the lives I am a part of. I'm nothing, but I'm everything. And for a second I was outside of it all. I saw it all, dude." He wasn't the least bit agitated, speaking in a tone that was unnervingly incisive.

"Um, sure thing, buddy. You want some water?" I didn't want to mock him by pretending to comprehend exactly what he was talking about.

"No, I'm not thirsty. I just want you to understand. Maybe if you can understand what I'm talking about now then you can tell me later. Because I know the second this wears off I'll lose it all. I've been blessed with this moment of insight. I'm free right now. Free from fear." He had his hands on my shoulders, eyes unblinking and refusing to let me look away. But it wasn't fear of Mack hurting me that made me stay; I genuinely wanted to understand what vision had made him transform like he had.

He saw my hesitant desire and blinked a couple of times to regain his focus, desperately grappling to find the right words to express what he had discovered..

"Muff, dude. There are other universes. Never feel trapped in this one, because there is another where you are free. I know this is all you know, and it will be all I know once this wears off, but it's not all there is." His body trembled with the passion of his words, the power of his conviction. "Don't fear death and don't fear life. I've finally *seen* myself, and it's so liberating. If I could live my life with this knowledge I would never be lost. But it's not meant to be." He took his hands off my shoulders and shook his head repeatedly. "It's not meant to be." He gave me one last burning glance and walked back to the room.

He passed out on the couch looking at the rug. The next day I casually asked him what he remembered from the previous night.

"I remember seeing something. But it's all kind of fuzzy. I really felt comfortable though, like I was at peace. I dug that. Not sure I want to do it again. Finn said Tom freaked out hardcore. And Pete said he is a little suspicious of lamps now. Maybe I got off easy, right?"

"Yeah, maybe."

Now, three years removed from college, lying in my bed, I had a realization on par with Mack's. I saw my life, I saw my dissatisfaction; I saw my desperation. I was clutching those sleeping pills, hoping for a release. But what would happen to me if I granted myself that release?

Was there another Sam who would decide against it and continue to live? Where would that Sam go with his life? What decisions would he make? Could that Sam persevere, find a way to succeed on his terms? Or would he just keep on wishing he had decided to take the pills?

I had had a good life. I had no complaints. I tipped the bottle over and poured a dozen or so into my palm. I didn't want any more of this. That's one thing I knew for sure. I was so sick and fucking tired of this. A deep, resonant hatred had slowly sunk into my bones, poisoning my marrow. I was toxic. The only thing staying my hand was thoughts of Pete and the subway, and the horror of making a decision like this and then changing my mind as my remaining life ebbed out. But that fear wouldn't delay my verdict much longer.

Keys jingled in the lock of the front door. My reflexes were slow, but I still managed to toss the pills and Belvedere back into my nightstand drawer before Mack poked his head in.

"Muff, you look nervous. Did I just interrupt a nice whack session?"

"No, just thinking about shit." I did my best not to slur.

"Okay, whatever. Well, it was a nice service. Finn read a poem in your place."

That was surprising. "Finn? Really? Since when is he a poet?"

"Yeah, I didn't know he had it in him. It was good though. Brought back good memories of Pete."

Enough of that. "Okay, cool, so you got that big date tonight? Ready?"

Mack shrugged. "Yeah, I guess. I hope she's as hot as I remember."

"That's the spirit!" I pulled myself off the bed with great effort and waved for him to get out. "Now go get 'em buddy!"

His nose twitched a little upon smelling my breath. "You get drinking without Finn?" He gave a quick glance around the room. "I don't see any booze."

"I thought I would get a head start." I didn't like concern in Mack's voice. He was the fucking alcoholic. I put my arm around him and steered the two of us out of my room. My decision would have to wait until another night.

We entered our living room to find Finn on the phone with his parents, letting them know about his acceptance to Duke.

"Yep. The financial aid covers half of it. So I'll be in debt, but better off than most. I'll be leaving Boston in a month or so. It'll be good to leave this city behind. Living here was getting a little stale. I could use a change of pace. Although I'm sure I'll be too busy to be social."

I stopped listening after that. I walked over to the fridge and took out a pair of beers, tossing one to Mack and opening the other for myself.

"To your date!" I yelled, immediately chugging half of it. Mack looked a little off-put by my aggression, but obliged me and took a big gulp.

"Muff, I never asked, but what happened to your lip?"

I had forgotten about that. I reached up and felt it. Still a bit swollen.

"Fell down night before last after I came back from the bar. I was pretty wasted."

He laughed. "You just took a digger and landed on your face? I wish I had been there to see that."

"Yeah, I got some looks at work yesterday. I don't think it really matters though. My days there are numbered anyway." I explained to him my email situation, finishing up right as Finn came into the kitchen.

"Are you fucking kidding me?" he exclaimed, having overheard from the other room. "You emailed that to your boss? Jesus Muff, what do you think is going to happen?"

"I don't know. I'll find out Monday. And if I get fired I'll find something else. Plenty of corporate jobs in the city."

"Still, that's bad news, man. Sorry to hear."

"Yeah, shit luck," Mack added. "But you'll find something. You're a smart guy."

I didn't want something. I wanted out. "Yep, I'll be fine. It was a shitty job anyway. Finn, catch!" I grabbed another beer out the fridge and launched it at him. He deftly snagged it and gave a quick examination.

"PBR? Come on, we can afford better than this."

"Don't be a bitch. It won the blue ribbon. It's great. Now, let's have a toast." I raised my tall boy into the air and waited for my roommates to follow suit. Once our beers rested against each other I began.

"Alright guys, it looks like our time together in Boston is winding up. We got a month left. Let's enjoy it. We've definitely had an interesting run, and if I could do the last seven years over again I would rather have no other friends by my side."

They both looked touched and a little awkward.

"And Pete. To Pete," Mack said solemnly.

"To Pete!" Finn and I answered in unison. We all drank deeply.

Mack left soon after to make his date. Finn and I polished off a couple more before heading out to meet some friends downtown. Despite being immersed in a social atmosphere I kept to myself, unable to displace the feelings I had been indulging earlier. I wanted no part of this.

I ordered us both a tequila shot and promptly retreated to a corner booth when some of Finn's friends from the lab showed up. There I stayed, leaving only to order more drinks. I'm sure I looked pathetic, but I could care less. I was tanked. At one point Finn came over.

"Dude, stop moping. It's a Saturday night. Tons of folks having a great time. Why don't you partake?"

"Nah," I mumbled. I was beginning to have a hard time staying awake.

"Come on, Muff!"

"Hey, good job on medical school. Now go away." I meant to say this, but it came out like I had a mouth full of oatmeal. He got the gist though, rolling his eyes as he left my booth.

I spent the rest of the night browning out. Somehow I got a cab back with one of Finn's friends from work, and somehow I ended up in my bed. I woke up at some point in the night and crawled to the toilet, making it just in time to vomit in its bowl. The one thing I remembered clearly the next day is how cool and refreshing that porcelain felt on my cheek as I rested my face there. My morning abruptly began with Mack's date hitting my head with the bathroom door, eliciting a groan from me and a surprised yelp from her. I made sure to apologize before dragging myself to my own bed. Wouldn't want to make a bad first impression.

20
BLOODY SUNDAY

I POSSESSED A single purpose when my eyes opened early Sunday afternoon. I had one reason for getting out of bed, for swallowing my nausea and forcing down some water: Lucie Mallory and the uncertain potential that she represented.

Something sinister was building inside of me. I wasn't quite sure when it had begun, maybe with Pete's death and maybe the moment I had left for Boston, but in recent months it had become a crescendo, a maddening buzzing in the back of my mind. I understood two things about this buzzing. It was there for a reason. It had been necessitated by my current situation. And if I didn't do anything to address it sometime in the immediate future it would drive me insane.

This was exactly why I had to call Lucie now. I had to know where we stood. Finding her name on my phone, I pressed send and began to rapidly tap my foot. It looked like I was the only one in the house. Good.

On the fifth ring she picked up. I was already thinking about how to leave a non-committal message when I heard her voice.

"Hi." Her voice sounded just as cute on the phone. I paused for a split second to collect myself.

"Hey Lucie, what's up?"

"Nothing much. Just about to go for a jog. How about you?" "Just...waking up." She laughed.

"Man, you really capitalize on your free time, don't you?"

"I do what I can." A pause. "So you want to chill tonight? Grab a bite to eat after you've worked up a nice appetite from your run?"

"Sam..." she trailed off, choosing her words. I already didn't like where this was going. "Sam, I had a blast on Friday and I'm glad we did it, but I have a feeling you are looking for something more than I'm willing to offer."

"Hey, I'm fine just chilling out. I just think you're fun to be around." I was doing my best to contain everything churning around inside of me, and thus far I thought I was succeeding admirably. "Nothing too serious."

She sighed on the other end of the phone, skeptical. "Sam, I've had a crush on you for a while, I won't deny that. Last night was great, but I also got some insight into you and where you are. And I don't think you're in a good place." She left me a space in which I could insert a challenge to that statement, but I remained silent. I'd let her do the talking.

"Sam, I just got out of a serious relationship, one that I found sapped a lot of my drive to improve myself. I stagnated in it. This is the time of my life to grow as a person, to focus on my career. You're a great guy, and I won't rule out something in the future, but definitely not right now. We're just in different places—that much is obvious."

"But I thought..." I almost said "we had something." Almost. If I had I wouldn't have forgiven myself. She wasn't even saying we didn't have a chance, just that there wouldn't be immediate gratification.

The thing is, with that buzzing in my head, immediate gratification was exactly what I needed. Time was running out. I needed her to fix me, but that clearly wasn't going to happen. The only thing I could do now was dust myself off and try to gracefully exit the scene. Quickly, before I lost control.

"Are you okay, Sam? I'm sorry if I led you on. I tried not to."

"No, hey, fun was had. No hard feelings. You go on that run. I might do the same. Beautiful day outside."

"Okay, well I'll see you at work on Monday, right? And we can still be friends."

"Definitely. See you tomorrow. Take it easy, Lucie." I didn't wait to hear her goodbye, immediately throwing my phone across the room. It hit the far wall and shattered, the sound violent and harsh in the silent house. I might be able to put it back together again, but I couldn't care less right now.

I slumped onto the kitchen floor, my back against some cabinets. Staring straight ahead, I saw a figure come into view. I didn't focus my eyes on it, but I knew it was Finn. He walked up to my slumped frame and nudged my foot with his own.

"Problems, buddy?"

"Things aren't going to work out with the girl I hooked up with on Friday." I said this in a dead voice, masking the anger still smoldering within.

"You can't catch a break, huh? Mack saw her, said she was cute. I don't know if she was worth breaking your cell for, but that's your call, not mine." If he meant the last bit to be funny I wasn't going to laugh. There was an awkward silence before he realized he would have to try a little harder to get me off the floor.

"Okay, Muff, let's shoot some hoops. Mack's at the grocery store, so when he comes back he'll play. I'll give Tom and Ben a call. Maybe Adam too? That'll make it three on three." He gave me a questioning look.

I was about to say no when I thought of a month from now, when there would be a day like this and I wouldn't be able to play with either of my roommates. That was just enough motivation.

"Yeah, sure. But no Adam."

"Come on, Muff. He's alright. And we might need him for even numbers."

Finn seemed to understand why I disliked him so much, but he himself couldn't summon up the same disgust. The reason I knew all too well. Finn's worst qualities, aspects of his personality that he rightfully muted, were traits the Adam loudly trumpeted, and on the basketball court was where the full extent of Adam's douchebaggery was displayed. Unfortunately, our friends Kyle and Johann had moved away in the past year, meaning that Adam had more chances to hang out with us.

"Fine. Whatever. He's not on my team though."

*****

It turned out everyone could make it, including Adam. Tom and Ben were still on their way, so the four of us shot around while we waited.

Adam was the tallest of us all, a well-built six foot five with close-cropped brown hair that highlighted his classic square-jawed features. A handsome kid, and he knew it. He had the ball and did a couple crossovers before draining a ten-footer.

"So, Duke, Finn? Not bad, not bad. And Mack, you're going to work for your daddy's bank? Does that mean no more temping?"

Mack also didn't like Adam, a mild grimace giving his feelings away. "Yeah. I start in a month. Should be a good opportunity."

I was under the basket, dishing Adam's ball back to him after he made his shots. He hadn't missed yet.

"How about you Sam? How's the job going?" He made another, this one a three. I tossed the ball again.

"I think I might be fired on Monday. Accidentally sent my boss an email ripping on him." That confession caused him to miss his next jumper. I got the rebound and fed him for a layup. He made it and passed it back.

"You serious? That's a dumb way to go out."

I took a shot and made it. "I know, right? Pretty retarded of me." I failed at keeping the sarcasm out of my voice.

Adam laughed. I don't think he had any idea how much I despised him.

"What do you think you'll do now?" He asked this with the curiosity of one who had never been in a position remotely resembling my current one. "If you get fired?"

I took another shot and clanked it off the back of the rim. "I don't know. I might leave Boston, try out a different city. Maybe go West Coast."

He gathered up the rebound and held the ball a second. "The way I see it, it doesn't matter where you go. It's all about what's inside you, not your environment. Like your friend Pete. Finn said he went out West and he didn't do well at all, so he came back. It didn't matter where he went, he was still unhappy right? If he killed himself surrounded by his friends, why wouldn't he have done the same thing somewhere else? It seemed like he couldn't escape whatever problems he had."

My whole body went taut. Just like that, I had a reason to care about something. I sharply jerked my head to the left, where Finn lay stretching.

"Hey Finn, you told Adam about Pete's time out West?"

"Yeah, I mentioned he had it rough out there. Just a few months ago. Not when he was alive. I know he didn't want us to." He said this looking at the ground, feeling my accusing stare. I believed Finn, but I still didn't like it. I imagined Finn and this fucking kid condescendingly discussing Pete and white-hot rage sizzled. I looked to the right and saw that Mack was aware how worked up I was. His eyes were wide, and he hesitated before taking another bite. He was eating a huge meatball sub right before a basketball game. I would have laughed at another time.

"Hey, Sam, calm down, I was just saying my piece," Adam interjected into the silence. I hadn't forgotten Adam, and I did my best to push every emotion down when I turned back to him. I think I partially succeeded, because he only looked a little put off. "It just seemed like he wasn't cut out for life after college. I didn't really know him, but I thought he was a nice guy. I was just trying to say how you shouldn't be leaving Boston just because you think another city will make life easier. Because it won't."

Who the fuck was this guy? Before I had time to answer we heard a shout and looked over. Tom and Ben had arrived, saving me the trouble of mustering a civil response. Since Finn knew I wouldn't be on a team with Adam, he took charge and divided up the six of us. Ben, Adam, and Finn would be on one team. Tom, Mack, and I were on the other. As the next tallest guy on the court, I would be guarding Adam. Awesome.

*****

I probably shouldn't have been playing. I should have said I wasn't feeling good and gone home, because the burning desire to cause Adam harm didn't go away when we started playing. In fact, it got worse, because basketball accurately reflects the personalities of those playing it. Passive people tend to avoid getting physical, while aggressive people are more than willing to use their bodies to their advantage. Depending on matchups, there can be room for both styles in a pick-up game. But when the less physical player (me) has to cover the more physical player (Adam), it's a disaster. He was dominating me down low and making sure to gloat after each basket, unable to resist mocking my inability to stop him.

After Adam's fifth straight basket, Mack offered to cover him. This was said quietly to me to avoid my losing face, but it still stung. I shook my head no and he shrugged, allowing me my pride. I hadn't said a word, but my heart raced and my head pounded. Getting abused like this on the court, regardless of who was doing it, would suck. That it was Adam, who represented so much I hated, focused my rage like a laser beam. I decided to fight back.

Finn dribbled around a pick Adam set. I expected Adam to roll, which he did. Finn quickly dished to his friend and I moved over to cover the star of the game. He grinned at me, the cocky smirk of one who is certain of success, and drove to the lane.

I did it so quick everyone missed it except for Finn, who had a great view of the play from where he stood. Right when it looked like Adam had blown by me I threw my elbow up. It looked from a distance like I was getting my arms up to block the shot, but a closer inspection would reveal my true intent. The sharpest part of my body collided with the soft flesh of his nose. I felt it give way and heard him cry out. Surprise, motherfucker.

He let go of the ball and dropped to his knees, hands rising instinctively to his face. I backed away, hands in the air, pretending innocence.

"What the fuck, dude?!" Adam yelled as his blood seeped through the fingers of his hand.

"It was an accident. Sorry." The apology sounded weak coming out of my mouth, and that's because I meant it to be. I wasn't going to fake remorse towards him. I wasn't going to pretend anymore.

Adam jumped up, seeing my lie for what it was. Now he wanted to fight and I didn't blame him. Under regular circumstances I would have felt exceptionally awkward. Just watching fistfights made me feel uncomfortable. But now? Now I wanted to mess Adam up even more. I wanted to dominate him, to make him feel the way I felt. Helpless and scared. How was it that people like him were the blessed ones? I bet he slept like a baby every night while I woke up in cold sweats. And why was that? Because he had "what it takes," that drive and ambition I lacked, the resilience which, absent in Pete, had apparently doomed him to his fate. Sure we did fine in college, but the "real world," that was where it counted. Where men like Adam and Finn succeeded and boys like Pete and I stumbled and fell. A perverse and sadistic joy surged through me as I observed a broken Adam. I wasn't completely powerless.

"You fucking piece of shit," Adam hissed, the venom dripping from his voice. He took his hands off his nose and began advancing towards me. Blood smeared over his face, nose possibly broken, he looked how I felt. I felt my hands clench into fists as I prepared to engage in my first fight since I was ten years old.

Then, just like that, I was on the pavement. Courtesy of Finn, who had given me a powerful and unexpected shove away from the approaching Adam. I lifted up my head and glared up at him, wondering if I would have to take both him and Adam on at once. But there was no anger in his face. Just sadness.

"Muff, go home. Leave right now and go home. Clear your head." He pointed in the direction of our apartment then spun back towards Adam.

"Sam, you think it's cool to pull shit like that?! I'm going to fuck you up!" Adam roared as he made to move around Finn and towards my vulnerable body. Finn stepped into his path and put a hand to Adam's chest.

"No, dude. I don't blame you, but it's not worth it. Let's get you to the hospital." Finn could be very persuasive, but I still expected Adam to knock him aside. Fortunately, he allowed himself to be pushed backwards by his friend, giving me one more stabbing stare before spinning around and walking off the court with Finn.

During all this, Tom, Mack, and Ben had stared, openmouthed and stunned. Once Finn and Adam left the court the spell was broken.

"Muff, I think you should do what Finn said. Go back to the apartment, dude." Mack said as he tossed the basketball, which was mine, over to me. He looked sad as well, but more confused than that. He didn't quite understand what Finn had the moment I elbowed Adam, didn't comprehend the depths of my frustration. I caught the ball and slowly raised myself to my feet. I was still angry, but more at myself than the world.

"Yep. Sounds good. Guys, sorry about that. I got a little too rough I think. Later." I looked apologetically at my three friends and they didn't respond, choosing only to nod their heads in acceptance as they struggled to maintain eye contact with me. I walked off the court and didn't look back.

21
FINN'S CONFESSION

LAYING ON MY bed in a fetal position, I embraced the silence of my room. I was too agitated to listen to music, leaving me with just the outside world as my sonic backdrop. It felt surreal, hearing the sounds of the neighborhood so sharply defined. Dogs barked, cars honked, mothers scolded their children, and I heard them. For a brief instant I felt connected to my surroundings, understanding that those around me shared the same world as myself. I shook my head and reached over to shut the window. Enough of that.

I curled up even more, tucking my hands between my legs. I would have loved to fall asleep, to escape from this. But I had only awoken five hours ago, making my usual getaway impossible. I could try to drink myself unconscious, but I had a suspicion I would just vomit up whatever I consumed. So I lay there, eyes closed.

Then I noticed it. I knew it was constantly there, but I wasn't always aware of it. The buzzing. Usually its emergence received an immediate response. This response, fueled by a terror of what it contained, consisted of me quarantining the unnerving sensation to a dusty attic in my brain. Then I was still cognizant but able to avoid giving it its due consideration. This moment, exposed on my bed, I had no protection.

I didn't want to put this off any longer. So I let it grow, let it spread to the entirety of my head. There, within the buzzing, corrosive thoughts took shape, devastating my perception.

Everything is nothing. You are nothing.

I realized my eyes were open, but I may as well have been blind. My brain had more important things to deal with then absorbing the visuals of the world around me.

All is lost. What you thought you had was illusion.

My heart began to strain and sweat beaded over every one of my body's pores. I must be having a heart attack, because no matter how hard I tried I couldn't stop the aching in my chest. Thank god I was lying down, because if I was standing I knew I already would have fallen.

Escape! But where would you escape? There is no escape.

I felt my body jerk once, and then again. I didn't recall asking my muscles to contract, but there they went. The spasms traveled up and down my entire body, from my grinding teeth to my curling toes. Now I begged for sleep, because no nightmare I could encounter would be as bad as this.

Through the haze of terror I heard a voice; saw a shadow block out the light. The voice got louder, becoming barely audible. Then I felt a hand grab my shoulder and spin my body around.

"Dude, answer me!" Finn was yelling as he shook me. "What the hell is wrong with you?!"

I moved my lips, but no words came out. Seeing Finn had broken me out of my trance, but my heart still trembled and my limbs remained leaden. After a few seconds a bunch of words spilled out in rapid succession.

"Canyougetmesomewater?"

Finn looked at me for what seemed like an eternity. He studied me, held my fevered eyes with his own. Then he nodded his head.

"Yeah, sure. I'll be back in a second."

After a minute or so he returned with a glass of water in one hand and something else in the closed fist of his other. I felt like I would regurgitate the liquid, but I did ask him to get me it. The least I could do was wet my mouth. With great effort I reached for the glass, only to have him pull it away slightly.

"Sam, you should probably take these with the water." Finn held out his closed fist, and when he saw my eyes focus on it he let his fingers relax and open. Two white pills lay on his palm. I was in no position to argue, so I did as he said, taking them down in one quick gulp. I mumbled my thanks and went back to staring at the ceiling, trying in vain to sharpen my gaze onto one particular place on its water-stained wall. I couldn't do it. And I couldn't stand still any longer. I had to move. I was twitching more and more, and the only way to cover it up was to start walking. I quickly rolled my body off the side of the bed and made to move towards the door.

"Sam, stop." Finn stood between me and the entrance to my room. I had built up some momentum in my steps towards the door and, as I stood in front of him, I couldn't help but jump up and down a little. My life was flashing in front of eyes and it was nothing. Life was oblivion. I was alone and my time was running out.

"Sam!" I jerked my head up, eyes wide. Finn put his hands on my shoulders and waited. He looked like he had something important to say, so I stopped moving long enough for him to talk. Satisfied, he began.

"I'm not going to let you out of my sight. If you want we can go for a drive or something, but you're not going to be alone like this."

"Finn I...things aren't good. I'm in a bad place right now. I'm in a real bad place. I got to get out of the house, out of the city." Unexpectedly, he nodded his head in understanding.

"Okay. I know what you're saying. I've been where you are. So trust me when I say in a half an hour you'll feel a lot better. Those pills I gave you will take the edge off, let you think clearly." He seemed pretty confident and I wanted to believe what he was saying, so I paid close attention. In the kitchen I could hear Mack on the phone with someone, planning out his night. With his new job at the bank lined up, the next few weeks would be prime drinking time.

Finn looked over his shoulder in the direction of Mack's voice and then back at me. He seemed to come to some sort of decision.

"Let's jump in my car anyway. It's a nice afternoon and we'll get some fresh air." It was more a command than a request, so I followed him out the door to where his beat-up Honda was parked. Finn was right; it was a really nice afternoon.

*****

We drove in silence for awhile, some undecipherable tune quietly filtering out of Finn's speakers, only to be swallowed up by the wind streaming over the open sunroof. Eventually, it dawned on me that I was no longer shaking. The tension in my body had ebbed out, leaving me remarkably tranquil as I watched the suburbs of Boston flow by. My mind seemed to accept that it would be unable to disturb this deep state of relaxation, and the hellish thoughts I had possessed faded as well. Finn must have sensed the angst fade, because he spoke as we stopped at a red light.

"Before I say anything, here's your cell," Finn took my repaired phone out of his pocket and put it in my palm. "As good as new."

I looked at it, touched that he had fixed it.

"Thanks man. Nice of you."

He shook off my gratitude and paused, gathering his thoughts. "Sam, I don't usually talk about this kind of stuff, but I have a feeling you're going through a rough time right now. Am I right?" I looked over and nodded my head.

"You could say that."

"I figured. What you don't know is that I went through the same sort of thing last summer. At least I don't think you know. You didn't, did you?"

I shook my head. Where was Finn going with this? I was already skeptical of what Finn's "rough time" entailed. He scratched at his arm, looking fascinated with whatever was there to be scratched, and began.

"So, I was studying for the MCATs in April when Pete died. That night we went to the Attic was actually the only time I had felt relaxed for a couple of months." He briefly went silent, and I assumed he felt the same weight as I did upon the mention of that night. It was funny though, I had largely forgotten how busy Finn himself had been while Pete had been writing. Pete's book and the aftermath of its completion completely overshadowed everything else.

"Yeah, so I had the test and my last-minute studying to keep my mind off of it, but when the day of the test came, something happened." The light had turned green without either of us noticing and the car behind us honked. He waved out the window and pulled forward before continuing.

"I choked. All those countless hours studying meant nothing, because when I sat down to take it my mind was like a sieve. I couldn't remember and I couldn't focus. I just stared at the page in front of me and felt like I was going to vomit. After fifteen minutes of that I forced myself to start writing, thinking it would begin to flow. But it didn't. I could recall the basics, but so much of what I had learned was just...gone."

"Yikes." I felt like I should say something. He nodded his head in acknowledgement.

"This was my second time taking it, and if you remember I was taking it again because I didn't get nearly a good enough score the first time around to get into a school like Duke. But I knew this one was a lost cause. I voided it so no school could ever look at the score and I walked out. I went back home to our apartment and I cried the whole afternoon."

I tried to imagine Finn crying and I couldn't do it. He had told us that night that the test had gone well, but that he might take it again just for insurance. And now he was in Duke. So what had happened?

"I remember telling my parents the next day and them being supportive." He said this rapidly, eager to move past this part of the story. "They said I must have just put myself under too much pressure and to take my time before trying to take it again. I agreed with them. So I waited a few weeks and tried my best not to think about it. It killed me though, knowing that I had just bombed the biggest test of my life. I felt like I was being eaten up inside. After those few weeks I signed up to take it in August and hit the books again." Looking agitated, he pulled the car into a school parking lot and put it in park. He glanced at me to make sure I was still with him. Of course I was. This was the most Finn had ever opened up about personal stuff and I was riveted. Letting loose a rueful sigh, he resumed his tale.

"Bad idea on my part. You get three initial chances to take the MCATs, and after that you can get special permission to take more. But I wasn't thinking of the chances I still had left, I was fixating on the probability of me choking again. I thought about Pete a lot as I stayed up studying. How he had had it all and then, just like that, the rug had been pulled out from under him. If it happened to him, why couldn't it happen to me?" He sounded confused even now as to how exactly Pete had been struck down. I wasn't confused, but that was only because I was walking the same tightrope.

Finn shook his head. "I knew I wasn't Pete, but it still terrified me. My dream had always been to be a doctor like my dad, and if I couldn't get through my mental block, it was going to be next to impossible to get into any of the schools I wanted to get into."

"Man, I had no idea. You should have said something. Vented to me and Mack."

Finn laughed, but without any bitterness. "You and Mack? As far as Mack goes, he's a great guy and he's like a brother to me, but he doesn't understand what it's like to be tortured by your own ambition and failure. This is a guy who still hasn't had a full-time job or any real responsibility in his life. He's never really tried, and because of that he's never really had a chance to fail. His solution would be me getting hammered and finding some chick to fuck, and if somehow that didn't solve my blues he would probably just tell me to ask you for advice."

I couldn't object to that.

"As for you, Muff, I think you forget what you were like for the first few months after Pete died. You drank a ton, read *The Valedictorians* like a dozen times, and that was pretty much it. You were not at all aware what was going on outside your own world. And to a certain extent you're still caught up in your own shit because of Pete dying." Seeing me start to open my mouth in protest he cut me off.

"No dude, you're not a bad friend, and I know if I came to you, you would do your best to hear me out. But you were oblivious to those around you. I'm not blaming you, because I have been really self-involved too. I mean, it's only recently I've been realizing that you might be in worse shape than you let on."

I debated voicing my disagreement to this statement as well when I considered the events that had led to me being in Finn's car. Probably best to shut up and let him resume his story, which he did upon seeing I had nothing left to add.

"So, yeah. Crippling self-doubt. And I couldn't sleep. I just kept on imagining where my life could be in a worst case scenario, and no matter what I did I couldn't shake out of it. Then, what started in my head started affecting my body. I would wake up immediately on edge, and the rest of the day I stayed that way. I was a live wire. I would go on ten mile runs and it wouldn't be enough. Sometimes it would get really bad and I felt like I was going to die. My heart would hurt and I was sure I would suffocate. Finally, in July, a really bad case happened. Remember when I said I got really sick at work and had to go to the hospital?"

"Yeah. You looked like shit when you came back."

"I'm sure I did. I basically had what I thought was a heart attack. But when the doctors had a look at me they told me nothing was actually wrong with me. That's when I knew something was really wrong with me. They thought that maybe what I had was an anxiety attack brought on by stress in my life, and that I should go see a psychiatrist."

"Wait, you were seeing a shrink? You? For how long?" I couldn't possibly fathom Finn sitting in a leather chair sharing his hopes and fears. This whole conversation should have been adding to my agitation, but thankfully Finn's pills had surrounded me in a bubble of calm that it seemed nothing could disturb.

"I just stopped seeing Dr. Nelson a few months ago. She prescribed the Xanax you're currently enjoying. I knew I was in no state to ace the MCATs. I was barely going to be able to keep my job at the lab the way I was functioning, so I went to see her a couple of times a week and talked it out. She really helped me take a step back and identify what was messing with my mind. You know what the root of it all was?"

I assumed this question would be answered by Finn. It was.

"The root of all this was just my perception. Our perception. We came from Fulton, a tiny insular school that shielded and protected. It laid out all our choices neatly in front of us. You have these choices for classes, these options of countries to go abroad to study in. You'll be eating your meals here and you'll have this area to live in. Then that umbrella is gone and we realize that we've been in the middle of a hail storm the entire time. So we sprint for cover somewhere to avoid getting pelted."

Finn stopped to let his words sink in. He wasn't one to use extended metaphors, but this one had been ironed out extensively. There were few things I appreciated more than a well thought out metaphor. I nodded my approval.

"They tell us when we graduate that the world is ours. We have just gotten one of the best educations money can buy and can use it no matter what path we decide on. The problem is that there are so many paths to choose from and that hail is coming down, making our first decisions half-assed ones. So, we panic and choose the most convenient shelter. Not the one we would prefer, but the one that's the easiest to get to. It's a natural reaction. The problem comes when we decide we won't risk the hail again, but the truth is that we should be more afraid of rotting in a hole then we should be of taking a couple of bits of hail."

He was getting very animated now, completely shedding any of the cool, detached demeanor he typically wore as his armor.

"So that's what I did. I left my shelter, went out into the storm, and accepted that life is risky. I could fail. But, I also realized there were other paths I could take if I failed at being a doctor. I also came to the conclusion that I really did want to be a doctor, so I should go for it." I recognized the resolute tone in his voice; his words now contained the confidence I typically expected him to project.

"I mean, this whole process took months for me to complete, but that first instant I left my comfort zone and accepted that I didn't have to be a doctor I felt free again. It was like a weight was lifted from my shoulders."

Sounded nice, but I wasn't going to be convinced that easily.

"So, it worked for you. You're a driven kid who had a concrete goal in mind but who just had to put it all in perspective. But what about Pete? He went to California. He went out of his comfort zone. Looks like he couldn't weather the storm." My voice caught in my throat and I coughed quickly to cover it up. I looked hard at Finn and that exuberant expression disappeared, but he didn't hesitate in responding.

"I thought about that a lot too. Pete had more options than any of us, but Pete didn't want to accept that the umbrella we had been blessed with was temporary. That didn't mean he had to get messed up by the storm, but that's the way he saw it. Either be miserable, locked into a life that was safe but stale, or give up and accept that things could never be what they were at Fulton. He had a crippled worldview and as long as he clung to it he could only be unhappy."

Interesting theory.

"Okay, so you paint this picture of countless opportunities being laid out in front of us. Easy for you to say as you start working for your MD. Whenever I try to think of other careers I could pursue, I always come up empty. Maybe I actually don't have any other shelters waiting for me. Maybe this one I'm in is the best I can hope for." I tried and failed to keep the spite out of my voice.

He gave me a neutral stare before responding.

"Muff, I won't deny that it might seem like there is no hope. I think your future has always been a lot more vague then mine, but that doesn't mean you won't have an amazing one. Like Pete, there's a lot you could do, but you have to want to chase it. I think you're too busy blacking out and hiding to seriously say you have given a long hard look at what adventures might await you. Try giving the real world the old college try, and I think you'd be pleasantly surprised by the results."

I didn't feel like answering immediately. And Finn seemed fine with that. So we sat together in his car, in that school parking lot, watching the sun slowly dip across the sky. A few minutes went by with the both of us silently staring ahead, savoring the infusion of spring into the world around us. Finn had made some good points, and his empathy was touching. He really did care about my welfare. But that didn't mean I was ready to muster up the energy to give a damn.

"We'll see, dude. I think I'm just in a bit of a down cycle right now. Good to hear you're doing better though, and thanks for being there." I reached over and clapped him on the shoulder in an effort to further show my gratitude. He looked unconvinced, but still managed a smile as he put the car into drive.

"Alright Muff, let's hope that's the case. I'm not saying it will be easy to get out of this slump either." He gestured to the scene outside of our car, one filled with kids in a nearby playground, couples taking walks together, and birds chirping their songs. "This existence is one big struggle to discover and hold onto the things that make it worth living, that make it greater than the death that awaits us all. The only way you lose is if you give up." He turned to me and grinned. "I thought up that profound statement one afternoon in the shrink's chair."

I laughed. "You've been doing a lot of thinking in general, haven't you? Really pondering shit? Because it shows."

Finn smirked as he pulled out of the parking lot and into traffic. "I'm just saying Muff, just saying."

*****

After Finn had driven me back he suggested Mack, he, and I go out for dinner. With most of my previous angst still neutralized by the Xanax I had agreed, suggesting this great BYOB place I knew in Brookline. As I walked down to the corner liquor store to pick up the beer I tried to focus on Finn's words to me. It was hard because his pills had also made me feel like someone had stuffed marshmallows inside my skull, but I decided it was important to try.

The problem wasn't the logic of what Finn said, it was its emotional relevance. I knew I had to *feel* what he was saying, and I had no idea how to let his message sink all the way to my core. Right now they were just pretty words, encouraging but fragile when applied to the nagging despair I held even closer.

I was jarred out of my reverie when my foot stepped over the curb and my body suddenly dropped. I stepped back onto the sidewalk and focused my eyes. Across the intersection I could see the liquor store, and I considered how many beers I would buy. Six-pack? Twelve-pack? Eighteen-pack? I was mighty thirsty.

This was a busy square, and a small group of people had gathered on either side of the street waiting for the light to change. I saw movement out of the corner of my eye. The man next to me was waving across the street at a pretty woman and her young daughter. The woman had luggage, and based on the excitement on the girl's face it had been a while since she had seen her daddy. Or maybe not—kids got excited about everything. I envied them so much for that ability. In her defense, her parents seemed just as enthused to see each other. Well, until the father's Blackberry went off and, driven by compulsion, he pulled it out of his pocket to discover what urgent message awaited him.

Children are impatient and clueless to the dangers that surround them, and this one was no different. Unwilling to wait another five seconds, the little girl jerked her hand out of the safety of her mother's and began running to the other side. Mom, not missing a beat, took a couple of efficient steps and reached down to sweep up her child. But she stumbled and fell, allowing her daughter to pull a few crucial feet away and totter into the middle of the intersection. The few other pedestrians on the sidewalk who had noticed what had unfolded in the past couple of seconds stared uncomprehendingly. The logical conclusion, being made obvious by an oncoming SUV still looking to make the yellow light, hadn't been grasped. Stomach clenching, I shot a look at the father. He was still staring intently at his little phone, soon to be awakened to the horror beyond him. In the next available moment I was moving, legs churning and hand outstretched. It was also in this instant that the mother abandoned her silence and let loose a wild scream of "Anna!"

Maybe the driver heard that scream. Or perhaps they saw the woman, reaching out to something in the path of their mighty steed. Whatever instigated the reaction, it was instantaneous. A spastic jerk of the wheel forced the vehicle away from both mother and child and directly towards the only other person in the street. In that extended half second I felt betrayed. I, for once, was trying to help another person, but before I could experience brief satisfaction at their salvation I myself was going to die. Without warning I would be cast out into the dark, unable to savor the good times or reflect on what lay ahead. But then, that's all I had been doing for some time, musing on my life in relation to death. And now, now that I actually faced a real, immediate end, I knew that I had blasphemed. I had imagined myself as a dealer of death, a steady hand prepared to pull my own plug and assert my mortality. Except this car was about to hit me, and that way of thinking now couldn't seem any more myopic.

I had struggled to grasp for so long exactly what had gone on inside Pete's mind when that subway bore down on him. No need to wonder anymore. I could only assume he was like me now: an infant, powerless, with any pretense of control dissolved. There was no way to make death your own. Whether it was by my hand or this careening Cadillac, it was all the same. It could have happened any time in the Fulton "bubble." I could have fallen down the stairs drunk and broken my neck or I could have choked in the cafeteria. I wasn't safe anywhere, and by opting out of life I wasn't exercising initiative, I was just speeding up the inevitable. I had never felt so liberated.

As quickly as they had leveled their steely gaze at me, the SUV's headlights looked away. Its side view mirror did slam into my shoulder, spinning me around and into the ground, so that I heard rather than saw the crunching metal when it careened into a telephone poll twenty feet away. Several seconds later I turned back around to see the dazed driver, blood streaming from her nose, stumble from her car and rush over to where the little girl lay unharmed, surrounded by her parents and onlookers. Gingerly rotating my right arm and experiencing throbbing pain from my wrist to my neck, I felt honored. The price for my deliverance had been a pittance. I breathed deep and reflexively closed my eyes, feeling every atom sizzle with life.

"Hey, you okay, dude?" It was the father, Blackberry now absent, looking me up and down before glancing back to his own daughter.

"Yeah, I'm gonna be alright. Things are gonna be okay." I laughed and felt guilty for doing so, but he didn't hold it against me, matching my carefree exclamation with one of his own before clapping me on my shoulder and jogging back. He was the only one who asked about my well-being, but I understood. I watched until the cops came and the crowd began to disperse, the whole time trying to get a handle on myself. What I had seen didn't address my frustrations with life, but it did give the perspective Finn had mentioned. And that's what I suspected I needed most, to take a big step back.

I turned and left the square, taking slow, methodical steps back to the apartment, alcohol forgotten. Eventually I got back and walked into the kitchen where Mack and Finn sat waiting. They both looked up and, noticing I didn't have the beer, asked why. I briefly explained what I had happened and received shocked exclamations of "You got to be kidding me?" and "Jesus dude, close call. You okay?" I nodded my head to confirm I was alright, not wanting to say anything else. We then made the bold decision to grab a couple of bags of chips and salsa and watch *Dazed and Confused*. We settled in, put our eyelids to half mast, and tried to forget the events of the day. I failed in doing so, but I was fine with that. If nothing else, I felt I might, with time, learn something from all this.

After the film wrapped up I informed my roommates I would be heading to bed early. I knew it was pointless to stay awake any longer, and my fervent hope was that I could have my thoughts sorted out when I woke up Monday morning. I didn't know if this was possible, but I did something unusual to help myself out.

As I made my way to my bed I stopped and knelt. Like I had done countless times as a child, I leaned my elbows onto my mattress and hung my head. A prayer of sorts. I expected no answer, and I received none. This wasn't for the God in the heavens, the one pulling the strings. This was for the God inside of me, the guide I had lost.

I held the position for a long while, saying nothing but asking everything. When I felt I had done all I could, I rose and crawled into bed. Sleep claimed me almost immediately. I had been up for less than eight hours.

22

RETURN TO DREAMLAND

I REMEMBERED THIS wallpaper. Blue stars and moons on a white backdrop. My parents never changed it, even after I went to college. I was on my side, facing it. Lying in my old bed, my feet hanging over the edge. I smelled bacon burning downstairs, heard the voices of my sister and parents talking in the kitchen. This was nice. I smiled and decided I would sleep a little longer. But wait—there was something else. The bacon wasn't the only thing that was burning. It was summer, so we wouldn't be using the woodstove, but I smelled burning wood. It started off as a faint smell, but it rapidly became much stronger. What the hell?

I rolled out of bed and walked to the window. Smoke filled my field of vision, but beyond that I could see flames. The woods around my house were on fire, tree after tree exploding into burning pyres. A deer, one of the many who would frequent our garden in the summertime, bolted through the blaze. It almost made it to our house before it too became enveloped. I turned away and sprinted across to the other side of the house. More flames there, as far as I could see. Now I ran down the hall to the stairs and the sounds of my family below. I had to warn them.

At the foot of the stairs I saw my little dog Buster, wagging his tail and barking frantically at his master. At least he knew something was up. But there was something wrong, and on closer inspection I discovered what. Buster's friendly brown eyes were gone, replaced by empty sockets, cold and black as coal. Before I could digest this I watched as his fur ignited like the trees outside and he scampered down the hallway, a barking four-legged torch.

Suspecting the worst, I crept one foot at a time down the hall to the kitchen, poking one eye around the corner to where the voices chatted. Yep, there were my parents and sister, having a leisurely conversation about how her day at school went. They had this casual conversation while they burned alive, blissfully unaware that their flesh was slowly melting off their bodies. It appeared I was too late to save them, but I was still going try.

The instant I stepped around the corner they became aware of my presence and ceased talking. Only now that I was there did the mood in the kitchen turn troubled, and I knew why. Unlike them, I didn't belong here. In my own house I felt like an intruder, the silence in the kitchen more suffocating than the smoke outside. I couldn't move. I knew they knew I was there, but I stood frozen as my family slowly turned and regarded me with their ruined faces. I wasn't afraid, and I understood they didn't expect me to be. They also didn't want me to feel welcome. Even with their countenances resembling melted candles I could discern that their expressions were hostile.

My father shambled a couple of steps over and threw up his arm in my direction. It almost seemed like he was reaching for me but understood that contact was impossible. Despite the horror of seeing him like this, I still wanted him to touch me. I desired for my dad to hug me and let me burn with the rest of my family. I sensed he was about to speak and I tensed. From deep within his burning frame, a voice emerged.

"GO."

The command was harsh. I flinched, but didn't move.

Again he spoke, this time with even more authority, with the wisdom of a parent who knows what's best.

"GO. LET IT BURN AND GO."

*****

Gone was my house and the fiery hell that had swallowed it. In its place was a lush college campus. Fulton. I lay sprawled on the lawn outside the library, surrounded by my friends. Everyone was there. Mack, Finn,

Nora, Kate, Tom, Ben, Johann, Kyle, Liz, and other friends I hadn't seen since we were all back together on campus. A perfect fall day. My friends' voices spun around my head, saying familiar things, sparking discussions that had already taken place. It didn't matter. I smiled, memories of my blazing home all but forgotten. We talked of the past, not the present.

"Remember when you and Kate convinced those freshman you were married and looking to swing?" Ben asked, a huge grin on his face.

We all laughed, including Kate, who was sitting above me and softly running her hands through my hair. Just like she used to when we were together. She had the most infectious giggle, high-pitched and completely at odds with her very adult look. Tall and slender with brown pixie hair, she always seemed older than the rest of us, especially me. She stopped laughing and looked down at me, her big blue eyes widening a little as she silently asked if I would like to tell the story. I winked, signaling for her to go ahead. She loved this story.

"We've all heard this one, right?" she posed this question to the crowd, who all nodded their heads enthusiastically. "Okay, just checking."

"Well, that night a bold young freshman had decided he had it in him to score a senior girl. Me. I saw him high-five his buddies as he made his way across the party to where Nora and I were sitting. We knew what was coming, and it was her idea to use the marriage bit." She gestured to Nora, who took a half-hearted bow. She looked a little preoccupied and I understood her restlessness. Where was Pete?

Kate continued. "So anyways, he comes over and asks me to dance. I say 'only if my husband says it's okay.' This kid is floored as I signaled across the room to Sam, who gave me a thumbs-up."

"I had no idea what she was doing, but I figured based on the look on his face it must be good," I replied.

"Good call there. So anyways, I start dancing real sexy with this freshman, and he's getting worked up. Somehow he forgot the marriage part though, so I reminded him. Then he has the balls to ask me 'are you happily married?' I looked at him and said, straight-faced: 'no, to be honest, things have been stale recently. You want to help us spice things up?' And he nods his head so hard I'm worried it's going to fall off."

Kate keeps on telling the story, but I already know it ends with her and me in a room alone with this kid. We get him to strip naked before ditching him. Great stuff. I had forgotten how much fun Kate and I had together. But as she tells the tale, my thoughts are of Pete. No one's mentioned him yet. I wait until she's done before asking.

"Dude, Pete's gone. He's not coming." was Tom's response.

"Gone?"

"Yeah, man. We're actually just about to leave too. We've stayed long enough as it is. It's time." To emphasize his point, he looked over his shoulder and into the distance. There, a trail of smoke was visible. I could almost smell the burning and see my house being consumed again. Apparently everyone else also knew the significance of the smoke, because people quickly rose to their feet and began to make their way away from the oncoming blaze. Mack reached down to help pull me to my feet.

"Come on, Muff. Time to go."

I shook away his hand. "No. I'm waiting for Pete."

"Pete's not coming. He made his choice." Kate said this as she leaned over me, concerned. Now everyone had noticed I wasn't moving and they gathered around, occasionally looking over their shoulders at the rapidly approaching smoke.

Finn walked over and knelt down beside me. "Muff, dude, you can't stay here counting on Pete to show. We don't want to lose you too."

I shook my head. "I've made my choice. He'll come, and when he does we'll catch up with you guys." Everyone exchanged worrisome glances, but they were too anxious about the firestorm to argue.

"Fine, dude. But if he's not here in a few, promise you'll run and catch up." Finn made sure to hold my eyes with his own, as if that would guarantee the truth out of me.

"Definitely. Will do." A blatant lie, but one that had to be told. Someone had to wait for Pete, and it made sense for it to be me. Kate sighed and knelt down beside me. She held my face in her hands, so delicate and smooth, and kissed me.

"I did love you, Sam."

I didn't know what to say to that, so I kept quiet and let my eyes convey my appreciation of that statement. She understood.

With that, it was decided. I was left at the foot of the Fulton library to wait. I could tell that no one believed Pete would show up, but they respected my wishes enough not to openly question them. Well, almost no one believed. As the group walked away, Nora held back for a second. From twenty feet away she pierced me with her gaze. She wanted to stay with me, to wait for him to show. But it was different for her than it was for me. My love wasn't hers, and I couldn't pretend to understand her longing. Her final choice was to follow the others, and I knew she thought it was the right one. I was inclined to agree with her. Me? I had unfinished business.

So I waited. I waited much longer than the "few" recommended by Finn. The air grew increasingly congested and I coughed more and more with each passing moment. I faced away from the fire, preferring not to see the campus burn behind me. I did not want to burn, but more than that I did not want to miss Pete if he decided to show. I would never forgive myself if that happened.

It couldn't have been far from the point of no return when I sensed another person lay down beside me. I turned, already smiling. The smile was returned by a singed, but still whole, Pete. I thanked God that he didn't look like my family. I don't think I could have handled a conversation with a melted Pete.

"Taking your time, I see." I coughed and wiped some moisture from my eyes. I could tell myself the tears were from the smoke, but I knew better.

Pete wiped his soot covered hair from his face, green eyes twinkling. "Yeah, well, I thought I would make you earn it. Nah, just kidding. I never doubted you buddy." "You left us kind of high and dry back there. You at least could have given notice that you weren't going to be along for the ride." There was no accusation in my voice, only sorrow.

"Yeah, in hindsight I think I might have done things differently. But hindsight is pretty useless when you're dead. Just an annoying thing which enhances regret. I would prefer not to dwell on my mistakes." He sounded really tired.

"Well you're here now. At Fulton! Pretty sweet, right?"

He nodded and smiled. "Yeah it is. Lot of great memories. And no regrets."

"Kate was telling everyone about the time we got that freshman naked so he could swing with us."

"Haha! I love that story!"

"I know you do." We were silent, the only sound being that of the crackling wood. The fire was close now. No time to waste.

"Pete, how about we leave now? Catch up with everyone else? We still can. Nora's up there too."

He paused and I tried to imagine he was giving it serious consideration. Then he shook his head.

"Nope, Fulton's where it ends for me. I made my choice already. Come on Muff, you know this." He was exasperated, looking pained as he spoke.

"Pete..."

He cut me off. "No, Sam! No! It's bad enough that I'm going to stay here, but what would be even more tragic is if you joined me. So please, just go. Thanks for waiting, but this is it."

"Fuck you, why?! Why, dude?!"

"Muff, it's really close now. You don't have time for this." His point was sharpened by the growing heat I felt behind me. "You owe it to me, you owe it to yourself. Leave me."

The wall came down inside me. I looked over my shoulder and saw the disintegrating campus, where flames raced across the lawn and from building to building. This is what he had resigned himself too. But not me. I was going to take my dad's advice. I was going to go.

I got to my feet and so did he.

"Take it easy, bud." I forced the words out. There was nothing else I could say at this point. He extended his hand and I took it.

"You too, Muff. And don't look back."

I turned and began walking away.

"Oh, and Sam?" I spun around, saw Pete silhouetted against the fire. Fulton burned, and soon he would with it. "Don't forget the book when you go. I'd like to think I did alright with that, and I don't think it's outlived its purpose yet. Also, I told you not to look back! Come on, man! You'll never make it in the world if you don't learn how to take direction!" He laughed, carefree in his final moments here, giving me a casual salute. I returned it before turning again and steadily walking away.

No looking back this time.

23

THE GREAT ESCAPE

NO LOOKING BACK.

I woke up with a gasp and immediately sat upright in my bed. My clock said seven. Seven o'clock, April 16th, 2007. It was time to go.

I packed quickly, filling two suitcases with clothes and essentials. Pictures of friends, my Frisbee, a couple seasons of *The Simpsons* on DVD.

When I had finished I gave one last look around. My eyes drifted back and forth, analyzing the contents of my room for anything critical I would need. Ignoring the obvious until I was sure I had missed nothing else, I finally let my vision settle on the worn copy of Pete's book. *The Valedictorians* lay on my nightstand, challenging me. Should I take it?

I didn't usually remember more than bits and pieces of my dreams. I knew I had had a nasty nightmare a few nights ago when I had pissed myself, but the specifics had since faded. This dream, however, I remembered every instant of, in crystal clear detail. The Pete in my dreams had wanted me to take his book. I would agree with dream Pete that he had done something notable when he wrote it, but I didn't have the slightest idea what I would do with it when I left. It seemed selfish to keep it all to myself, but who was I to disagree with the wishes of its author? I reached down and gently laid it in my suitcase. There. Now I was ready.

I made my way to the kitchen, hoping to see neither Mack nor Finn. I didn't want to have that conversation. Setting my suitcases against the kitchen table, I seated myself. Time to say goodbye. We left a pad of paper and pen on the table to leave each other messages, but never any message quite like this. I made it short and sweet.

> *Guys, I'm leaving Boston. I decided that it's time for me to mix things up a bit, and now's as good a time as ever. I've left my checkbook on the table. Take whatever you need for utilities or rent. Oh, and if Adam needs money for medical bills. I'll be off the grid for a while. I even deleted my Facebook profile! I don't know how long I'll be away, but I wouldn't count on me returning calls. Best of luck to both of you, and thanks for being the friends you are.*
>
> *Signing off,*
> *Sam "Muff" Orcutt*

That was that. I laid my checkbook on the table and made my way to the door. I stopped briefly, outside of Pete's room. When I looked in, all I could recall of my friend was the image of him saluting me on the burning Fulton campus. And that probably didn't even happen. I smiled and closed his door. Bye, buddy.

*****

As I drove through the suburbs on my way to the highway, I soaked in all the humanity around me. I couldn't hate it because there was no need. I had accepted that the confrontation wasn't with the outside world, but with me. Now I was thinking with a clarity I hadn't had in a very long time. I felt blessed, but not because I currently had a mind-bending sense of my own potential. Everyone felt that occasionally, passing moments of insight that hit you like a shovel and then disappeared a half hour later. Eventually, for a brief instant in time, everyone's neurons lined up perfectly.

I was grateful because I was doing something about it and ensuring the continuation of my self-empowerment. If you're having a moment of clarity, you can utilize it in one of two ways. You can appreciate its relevance to your current situation and run your mouth off to your friends about the knowledge you've been graced with, or you can apply it to your life and engineer a drastic overhaul of a situation you know needs to be altered.

I had woken up today with perspective. When I departed the realm of the unconscious, I entered a world drastically changed from the one I had previously existed in. Maybe it was the dream; maybe it was me almost getting run over; maybe it was Finn's kind words of advice. It didn't matter. I had been flailing about for almost three years, waiting for someone to throw me a life preserver. It was time I learned how to swim. I now possessed an unfamiliar momentum, and I savored every second of it. Every nerve in my body tingled like I was plugged into an outlet and was having currents of the sublime fed into me, but it still wasn't enough. It would never be enough anymore, that I knew. The search had begun.

My car hit the highway and I revved the engine, elevating my speed to match my mood. I opened my cell and made a call. Lucie picked up on the third ring.

"Hey Sam, what's up?"

"Nothing much. Just letting you know that if someone asks why I'm not there, tell them I officially resigned as of today."

There was a brief silence while she digested. "Are you kidding me? Is this a joke?"

"Nope, no joke. I'm done at Legacy."

"Just like that? Sam, are you okay? Is everything alright?"

"Lucie, everything is better than it has been in a long time. Trust me."

"Sam, I…"

"Lucie, you were amazing the other night. You really were. I will credit you with helping to kick-start my personal renovation."

"Um, thanks."

"No, thank you." And I really meant it. She was one amazing girl. "Okay, I gotta run. But just make sure to relay that message if anyone asks. Or maybe just type it up and staple it to Donald's forehead." She laughed despite herself.

"Alright, if that's what you want to do. Take it easy there, crazy man."

"Will do! Later days!" I hung up and focused my attention back on the road. I was almost up to the exit I would take to reach Legacy. There was still a chance to pretend it was all a joke, to face Donald's wrath and hope I could save my job. I could go back, pretend none of this had happened, and accept that life was as it was.

My foot hit the accelerator, pushing my car up to 100 by the time it passed the exit. A wild cry exploded from my lungs, carefree and proud. I hoped Pete could hear it.

It was time for a revival.

24

ONE MORE FOR THE ROAD

I HAD WANTED to go out. It was the second week of freshman year, and goddamnit I needed to explore. All the kids on my floor in Utley Hall had been satisfied with staying put and playing another game of beer pong, but I wasn't. I was drunk and ambitious.

For a school of less than two thousand, Fulton still seemed really big. I didn't know where to begin to stumble to, so I let my ears guide me. The first couple parties I heard were being held in upperclassmen housing and, while I fancied myself an adventurer, I wasn't a daredevil. I kept on walking. Now I was outside Franklin, a freshman dorm filled with my own kind. I listened hard, but no sounds emerged from within. Oh well. I started to walk by, only to jump a couple feet in the air when a barrage of laughter shot out of a basement window.

"Tom, man, that's some funny shit! She actually believed that?" I walked to the window, knelt down, and peered in. A group of a half-dozen boys were gathered in a circle as a pipe was passed around. They were all laughing at the dark-haired kid who was telling the story. Not exactly a huge party, but they looked like they were having some fun.

"Yep. I said that the Cirque de Soleil's bus was going to be leaving in a couple of hours, so that was all the time we had together. Unless she wanted to join us on the road," Tom responded to the questioner with mild bravado. A good-looking kid. I think he was in my Psych 101 class. Maybe that could be my in. I decided to venture down there.

So eager was I to join in that I almost tripped down the stairs to the basement. They must have heard me, because the laughter stopped. By the time I made it to the last step a half-dozen sets of red-tinged eyes were all focused on me. I started to make a motion to Tom, to ask him if he was in Psych 101, but my tongue caught in my throat. This was so awkward. I debated running back up the stairs and hoping none of them would recognize me the next day.

"Yo dude, what's your name?" The kid farthest away from me asked this. I had seen him around campus as well, shaggy haired and lanky. He always seemed to have a large group surrounding him, all of them interested in whatever he was saying. Now this group was interested in what I had to say. He smiled, hoping to encourage me to answer. He had a crooked tooth, something I found surprising.

"Sam."

"Hey, Sam! What's up, man? I'm Pete. Pleased to meet you. Want to take a seat, smoke up with us?"

"Sure." I had never smoked before, but now seemed as good a time as any to start. Pete pulled up a chair next to him and patted it, signaling me to join him. Just like that, the tension eased and everyone went back to laughing and talking nonsense. Once I was settled the questions started.

"You a freshman, Sam?"

"That I am."

"Me too! Where you living?"

"Utley."

"Utley! I've been there a couple of times. You know a kid named Ben who lives there? Third floor? Short guy, wears a lot of flannel?"

"Hmmm. I don't think so."

"Well, he's the man. Where you from, Sam?"

"Andover, Mass."

"Hey, I'm from Natick! You considering doing any sports while you're here?"

"Um, I've been going to some ultimate Frisbee practices." I was really thrown off here. I couldn't remember when anyone had taken such a visceral interest in me. Pete was acting like I was the only one in the room. His eyes sparkled, and he seemed genuinely engrossed in my halting answers. Man, no wonder people liked this guy.

"Disc, eh? I'm considering showing up to some of those practices. I played a little in high school and it was fun. All in all, you liking Fulton so far? Good classes?"

"Yeah, definitely. Awesome profs. Taking a couple philosophy classes I really like." That really seemed to set him off.

"Philosophy classes? Which ones? I'm thinking of majoring in philosophy."

"Already? Woah." I hadn't really thought about my major at all. "I'm taking Kantian Ethics with Pollard and…"

"Woah, stop right there! Pollard. How is he? Wait! Hold that thought. The pot's here." Apparently it was Pete's turn to take a hit from the pipe, and I was extremely grateful it was he rather than me. As a novice (I had only taken one hit off a joint at a party in high school), I planned on paying very close attention to how he did it. He put his thumb over the hole, inhaled deeply, held it in, and released the smoke through his nose, laughing as he did.

"Your turn, Sam." He passed it, as well as a lighter, into my tentative hands. I was pretty sure no one was looking at me, but I wasn't going to give myself away by looking up.

I steadied my grip and let the lighter's flame brush against the burnt plant within. When it began to catch fire I let my thumb lock down on that hole and proceeded to do my best Pete impression. I almost succeeded too, but my throat betrayed me and I began to sputter and cough. Pete laughed and the kid next to me took the pipe and lighter out of my possession.

We continued to talk, now both of us asking questions regarding the other. After a few more rotations of the pipe the conversation switched to girls. When it did everyone joined in.

"Hottest girl in the class?" Tom asked. "I'd have to say Nora, especially since I heard she just broke up with her boyfriend," The nodding heads around the room lent credence to his statement. "Pete? Your thoughts?"

Everyone switched their gaze from Tom to Pete, who was reaching the point of high where it was impossible to stop smiling. "Yeah man,

I agree. Nora. She's something special. I'm thinking of making a move now that she's single." I didn't know who Nora was, but this seemed to be a bold statement based on the impressed faces around the room.

"Really, Pete? Well, I was thinking the same thing." Tom tried to make a solemn face, but burst into laughter. He tried again and succeeded. "Seriously though, I want her real bad and I think I got a chance."

Pete looked over at his competition, squinting his eyes as he made a show of sizing Tom up. "Hey, don't let me stand in your way. We have four more years and I'm in no rush. But before we graduate I'll make a run at her, whether or not you're with her." He was smiling, but he was also serious. The confidence wasn't feigned. He was really into this girl.

Tom looked a little taken aback, but chose to laugh off Pete's sincerity.

"Alright man, I'll let you know how it goes. Best of luck to you as well."

Eventually we ran out of weed, and by the time that happened my head was like a hot air balloon. Beer seemed to materialize out of nowhere, only serving to further retard our brains. However, the drinks couldn't satisfy the growing hunger resulting from the pot, and soon kids were expressing their urgent need for pizza. One, a heavyset kid who looked like he was fifteen, told us he would take care of everything. He went upstairs an ordinary college student only to return a conquering hero. In his arms was a huge box, and within that box were muffins. Lots of delicious muffins.

"Mack! You're a legend!" Pete yelled as he ran up to clap the kid on the back.

Mack smiled and spoke, mouth already filled with muffin. "Homemade from my mom. Help yourselves."

We did. There were a couple dozen muffins total, and they were magical. The seven of us ate them all. I ate one, then another, then another, and so on. I couldn't stop eating. I was so hungry. I became terrified I would never stop being hungry, but by the time I got to muffin number six that crisis was averted. Only to be replaced by a new one.

Footsteps were heard at the top of the stairs and then legs appeared, descending down the steps. Security. In later years we would learn that the job of security at Fulton was to moderate the fun rather than to crack down on it. We would take pictures with them, offer them beers that they would good-naturedly refuse. But this wasn't then. This was the second weekend of our freshman year. We were scared shitless.

Except for Pete.

"Hey guys, what's up?" The instant he had heard the footsteps he had emptied out the pipe in the corner and put it in his pocket.

"Hey there. It's Pete, right? I believe we met the other night at that party at Wilson House?" There were two security guys, and it was a burly one with a mustache that said this. "You're really jumping right into things here, aren't you?"

He didn't miss a beat. "Yeah, that was me. Your name is Mike, right?"

The mustached one nodded his head and smiled at his partner before looking back at Pete. "It is."

"Cool. Yeah, well, I'm pretty excited to be here. So is everyone else. Right, guys?" He turned to us with an encouraging look on his face. We all nodded, except for me. I didn't want to move my head, worrying that if I did it would incite my stomach. Those muffins were not getting along well with the beer already there. Apparently the security guys noticed as well.

"Your friend, he doesn't look too well," Mike said, gesturing towards me.

"Oh, Sam? He's just tired. Long day. Sam, say hi." Pete's eyes widened a little as I got out of my seat, swayed a little, and made my way haltingly over to them. Things were really getting out of hand inside my belly, which felt like it was on a washing machine's spin cycle. It didn't help that the room wouldn't stop spinning.

"Hey…" my esophagus spasmed a little, and I stopped. When it had calmed down I continued my journey, hand outstretched. "My name is Sam. Pete's right, I'm not feeling very…"

Too many muffins. That was my last thought before my entire stomach emptied out its contents on the shoes of the two security guys. Chocolate chip muffins, blueberry muffins, banana muffins, all melding together in a beautiful, half-digested bake sale.

"Shit!" Both security guys yelled as they tried in vain to shake the vomit off of their feet. On my knees, I looked up at their livid faces and mumbled an apology.

"Sorry. Too many muffins."

I heard partially muffled snickers behind me, hinting at the out-of-control laughter that would certainly have happened were Mike and his partner not here.

Before either member of security could say anything, Pete stepped in.

"Stomach virus, I think. I'll take him back to his room and make sure he gets plenty of fluids before tucking him in." He pulled me roughly to my feet and began to drag me out.

"Muffins," was all I could manage as he pulled me up the stairs. I don't know why security let us go, but they did. I guess Pete didn't really give them a chance to respond.

The second we got outside I vomited again. And again. It felt just as good to expel the muffins as it did to consume them.

Doubled over a safe distance away, Pete laughed until he was incapacitated. His whole body shook as he collapsed onto the grass.

"The Muffin Man! Muff dawg! Muffy! Boy am I glad you showed up tonight."

I groaned and laid my body on the ground, exhausted from the exertion. "Thanks man. Nice to…meet you too."

"Fulton is something, isn't it man? All these people, one little campus." He said this more to himself than to me, staring up at the sky with a spellbound expression on his face.

"Yeah, it's great. Except for the muffins."

He laughed again, still overwhelmed with how funny it was.

"Muff, one day you'll master the muffin. Don't worry though. They'll be time for that and so much else. We have an eternity ahead of us." There was a pause where we both considered the future before Pete brought us back to the present.

"So honestly Muff, what do you think my chances with Nora are?"

"I don't know who she is, so… I think you got a great chance."

"Aww, thanks man. That means a lot."

We both lapsed into silence, observing the starry night. In the distance I heard kids laughing, projecting joyous, untroubled sounds that filled the air. A smile spread over my face as I realized how beautiful it all was.

A fart from Pete broke the quiet and we both laughed some more.

"Want to go find another party?" he asked.

"Yeah sure, the night is still young."

He got off the ground, helped pull me up, and we began our journey. Our destination was uncertain, but it's never about the destination.

Breinigsville, PA USA
04 December 2009
228631BV00005B/1/P